If
Animals
Could
Talk

If Animals Could Talk

William L. Coleman

BETHANY HOUSE PUBLISHERS
MINNEAPOLIS, MINNESOTA 55438
A Division of Bethany Fellowship, Inc.

Illustrations by Valery Larson Smidt.

Unless otherwise indicated, all scripture quotations in this publication
are taken from the Holy Bible, New International Version. Copyright
(c) 1973, 1978, 1984 International Bible Society. Used by permission
of Zondervan Bible Publishers.

Verses marked TLB are taken from *The Living Bible*, copyright 1971
by Tyndale House Publishers, Wheaton, IL. Used by permission.

Published by Bethany House Publishers
A Division of Bethany Fellowship, Inc.
6820 Auto Club Road, Minneapolis, Minnesota 55438

Printed in the United States of America

Library of Congress Cataloging-in-Publication Data

Coleman, William L.
   If animals could talk.

     Summary: Descriptions of the catbird, panda, leopard, and other
wonders of nature demonstrate spiritual truth and the validity of
living according to Christian faith. Biblical quotations follow each
passage.
     1. Children—Prayer-books and devotions—English.
[1. Animals—Miscellanea. 2. Prayer books and devotions.
3. Christian life] I. Title.
BV4870.C6324   1987   242'.62   87-7141
ISBN 0-87123-961-2

WILLIAM L. COLEMAN is the well-known author of nearly three dozen books on a wide variety of topics. Combining his vast experience as a pastor, researcher, writer and speaker, Bill is noted for his effective devotional writing in the area of family relationships. He has been married for over twenty years and is the father of three children.

Other Books in the Coleman Family Devotional Series

Animals That Show and Tell
Listen to the Animals
Singing Penguins and Puffed-Up Toads
Before You Tuck Me In
Counting Stars
Good Night Book
Sleep Tight Book
My Magnificent Machine
More About My Magnificent Machine
On Your Mark
Today I Feel Like a Warm Fuzzy
Today I Feel Loved
Today I Feel Shy
Warm Hug Book

Other Books on Special Family Topics by Coleman

Getting Ready for Our New Baby
Making TV Work for Your Family
Getting Ready for My First Day of School
My Hospital Book

Contents

When Animals Speak

Animals have always been master teachers. If we tune in to their "language," some will teach us how to care for our families. Others will tell us how to provide for the cold nights ahead. Birds will let you know when the seasons are changing. Even a lowly dandelion will show you how to hang in there and keep fighting back year after year.

Nature is tough. And it tells us to hold on and become winners.

If we listen carefully, animals will teach us about the God who created them. We learn about God the designer, God the engineer, God the veterinarian, God the gardener, God the nature lover. We will see a glimpse of how He loves, directs and cares—not only for animals but for us, too.

We can't learn everything about God from animals, but they do offer classes that are a big help.

Bill Coleman
Aurora, Nebraska

one

If Animals Could Talk

A serious problem occurred at the airport on Midway Island. Laysan Albatrosses built their nests too close to the airstrip. Not wanting to injure the birds, workers carefully caught them and moved the group to the Philippines.

That seemed like a safe distance—4,120 miles from the airfield. Farther than the width of the United States! But in less than thirty days the albatrosses had flown across unfamiliar territory, over the open sea, and arrived back at Midway Island.

If an albatross could talk, we would ask him a few questions. How could he navigate day and night, good weather and bad, and end up home again? What kind of special equipment did God give that allows an albatross such skill? If we could interview birds, they could tell us something about God's ability.

The ducks of Bali, Indonesia, for instance, could give us some neat information. Every year a man comes to them with a flag tied to a bamboo stick. Immediately twenty or thirty will begin following the man as he parades down the road. At the end of their trip they arrive at a rice paddy where the rice has already been harvested.

The ducks waddle into the field and begin eating bugs. After they have picked out all the harmful insects, they follow the man with the stick back home again.

Ducks could tell us something about trust. They know how smart it is to be good followers. We could learn something about following God by watching a white, feathery fowl waddle down a road.

Nature doesn't teach us everything about God, but we learn many lessons from things that are outdoors—animals, birds, rocks, things that grow in the ground. Ants teach us about working hard. Lilies tell us not to worry. Lions give us lessons in boldness. Sheep remind us that God thinks everyone is important. A thirsty deer panting by a stream reminds us that we need to let God satisfy our spirits.

Nature is busy talking to us about the reality of God. The animals have lessons to teach that we have not begun to learn. If the animals could talk, we would be amazed to know what God is like.

"But ask the animals, and they will teach you, or the birds of the air, and they will tell you; or speak to the earth, and it will teach you, or let the fish of the sea inform you" (Job 12:7, 8).

Tell three lessons about God from nature.

two

The Imitating Catbird

How many noises can you imitate? You can probably do a good train whistle or make a sound like a trumpet. If you practice, you might be able to talk like some of your friends, teachers or favorite television characters.

Maybe you are like the catbird. It's a gray bird with a black patch on its head and red markings underneath its long tail feather. It is only nine inches long and loves to imitate other birds. If you listen carefully on a moonlit night, you might hear a catbird or one of the birds it imitates. How did the catbird get its name? It sounds just like a cat meowing.

Catbirds are often fun to have in your neighborhood. They enjoy eating berries and cherries, but they also like to gobble down plenty of crickets, beetles and ants. This helps keep the insect population from getting out of control.

In the fall catbirds like to wing their way around the southern United States and Central America. Spring finds them rummaging around North America and southern Canada.

They are much like other songbirds except for this peculiar talent of mimicry. In midair they can sound almost exactly like a bobolink. They can also copy the song of the kingfisher, as well as its sound and method of flight.

These great actors are not limited just to birds. If you need a frog croak, the catbird can do it.

Each of us has our own way of imitating. We imitate our parents, animals or our neighbors. The Bible encourages us to imitate God. Not just to make noises but to love the way God loves, to share as God shares, to forgive as God forgives.

We all act like someone else sometimes. We don't want to forget to act like God many times.

"Be imitators of God, therefore, as dearly loved children and live a life of love, just as Christ loved us and gave himself up for us as a fragrant offering and sacrifice to God" (Eph. 5:1).

1. What can a catbird imitate?
2. How did it get its name?
3. How will you imitate God today?

three

Fooling Their Enemies

Life in the wild is tough and unpredictable. At any moment a hawk could swoop down and snatch up a tiny animal, a snake might gulp down a frog, or a bear could pull a fish from the water. To protect themselves and their children, many animals have developed unusual behavior to help keep their young safe.

No technique is more unusual than the one used by the killdeer bird. They have become excellent actors and have often fooled their enemies.

If an attacker comes close to a killdeer's chicks, the mother bird will move away from the nest. It will then begin to drag one wing and act as if it can't fly. In case the attacker doesn't notice, the killdeer will also make loud noises to draw attention away from the chicks.

Frequently the enemy will creep close to the mother, trying

to catch it. Suddenly the "injured" killdeer will dart into the air and escape the confused attacker.

Beavers may not be good actors, but their warning system works well. If danger comes close, the beaver beats its flat tail, making a slapping sound and sending its family diving for cover.

Marmots warn their young by a sharp whistle. The first one to see trouble gives off a terrible sound and everyone dashes for home.

When a mother bear senses danger, she will try to move her cubs and avoid a fight, if possible. Her method of carrying a cub may not be one we would choose. She grabs the cub's entire head inside her mouth. Without harming the animal, mother jogs off to a safer den.

Parents are in the protection business, too. That explains why they provide care, housing and food. Unlike animals, people can think through needs and figure out how to meet them.

It's much like the protection God gives us. He watches over us, guards us and provides the things we need. God cares what happens to us and usually sees to it that we are watched over.

"For the Lord loves the just and will not forsake his faithful ones. They will be protected forever, but the offspring of the wicked will be cut off" (Ps. 37:28).

1. How does a mother killdeer protect her chicks?
2. How does a mother bear carry her cubs?
3. How has God watched over your family?

four

Animal Love

If you ask some people, they would say that animals are just dumb creatures who don't know anything about love. But anyone who has had a pet or has watched animals in the wild knows how much love exists.

When a mother bear even thinks its cubs are in trouble, she immediately risks her life to save them. The bear will attack almost anything to protect her cubs. At that moment she is filled with compassion for her children.

Animal lovers believe there is much more than mindless instinct involved. Millions of cat lovers will insist that cats develop an attachment to their owners that they share with no one else.

A true story is told of a trapper who caught a female bear in his trap. When he arrived to capture the bear, he saw the bear's mate standing next to her. The male bear was hugging her and crying. The trapper says he never trapped another bear.

Stories about animals developing affection for cats suggest an unusual depth of feeling. The depression they have gone through after being separated from the cat suggests real emotion.

We could make the mistake of pretending that animals have the same feelings as humans. However, we may have made another error by thinking that animals have no feelings at all.

Some animals keep the same mate all of their lives. Wolves and foxes have a lifelong attachment for their spouse, which suggests how much they care.

If we say animals love each other, scientists will start arguing whether that could be possible. However, if we say that

"love" means animals care about each other, who can deny that? They feed one another. In some cases they even feed adopted children. Many animals teach their children to hunt, to hide, to swim, to pick bugs off each other's scalp. They understand separation and are happy to be reunited.

Animal love is not human love, but it may be love nevertheless.

Love might be hard to recognize in animals, but it is easy to see in Jesus Christ. Jesus cares what happens to us. That is why He lived, died and rose from the dead. He cares about you and me.

By believing in Jesus Christ as our Savior, we accept the love He gives us.

"Greater love has no one than this, that one lay down his life for his friends" (John 15:13).

1. Have you observed an animal caring for another animal?
2. Tell about the trapper who caught a female bear.
3. Tell about Jesus' love for you.

five

Bird Nest Soup

It's good to try new foods once in a while. I've eaten crayfish, turtle, kiwifruit, liver pudding and chicken gizzards. Someday I'd like to try alligator meat, squid or seaweed. Nature offers too much variety for us to limit ourselves, especially if we live in nations where food is plentiful.

One food I'm not sure I can eat is bird nest soup. No doubt it is a fabulous meal, because people are willing to pay $40 for one bowlful. It might even be healthful. Many Chinese love to down a good dish of it.

No wonder bird nest soup is expensive. The nests are hard to find and often the supplier has to climb on dangerous cliffs to collect even one nest. His goal is to find a swallow's home. Swallows hide in far-off areas.

If the searcher brings back a pound of top-rate nests, he is paid hundreds of dollars. The more considerate hunters try to avoid nests with eggs in them, but with so much money at stake some don't care what happens to the birds.

Understandably, the thought of eating a nest may not send your taste buds singing. Fortunately, people don't eat the entire nest. The cook scrubs everything until it is extra clean and saves the part people enjoy the most: the swallow's saliva. When completed, it looks like white strings but it's stiff and firm.

There's no point in describing the rest of this. It only gets stranger. Those who eat it insist that their skin and complexion improve as well as their health.

If you wanted to do something special to please God, collecting swallow eggs might sound like a great idea. He might be impressed with an expensive gift that you risked your life to get. But God isn't looking for riches or daring accomplishments.

What God wants from us is our obedience. If we live our lives by following Him, by being good, and kind and loving—doing everything that pleases Him—we are doing exactly what God asks us to do.

If you find an old abandoned swallow's nest, give it to a friend. Tell him it is a special treat. But if you want to serve God, simply obey Him. Find out what the Bible says and follow Him.

"To obey is better than sacrifice" (1 Sam. 15:22).

1. What is the most unusual food you have eaten?
2. Where are swallows' nests found?
3. Think of something you will do today to obey God.

six

Born to Eat

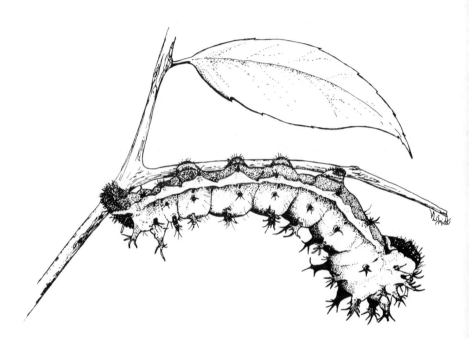

All of us enjoy a good meal. It's not only fun to eat but also essential to our health. However, there are some creatures, like the fuzzy caterpillar, that do little else but eat.

We know what caterpillars are. They are the fuzzy little creatures that later turn into moths and butterflies. On their way to adulthood caterpillars like to eat. Eating is their full-time job.

Many begin life as an egg placed on their favorite plant or leaf. When they hatch, the caterpillar will eat its egg and then begin its long journey of trying to munch on everything it can bite.

If the caterpillar finds itself hatched on a leaf that doesn't suit its appetite, the only solution is to move. It uses a silk thread as an elevator and drops rapidly to a plant where the food is more enjoyable.

This continuous eating is both good and bad. On the one hand, caterpillars help remove some overgrowth. Their eating provides an excellent product known as silk. But the caterpillar also manages to destroy millions of dollars worth of crops each year.

When you eat as much as a caterpillar, you are certain to have clothing problems. Their outfits soon become too tight and they are forced to discard their old clothes. This is called molting. Their outer skin falls off and the next layer takes over. The change in clothing could take place from two to ten times while they are caterpillars.

Even the change of clothes is special for some caterpillars. Often they will immediately eat the skin they have outgrown. If they're too busy for skinburgers at the time, insects might later have the clothing for dinner or it could merely blow away.

Unlike caterpillars, people are not born just to eat. We do many helpful and enjoyable things. A few of us fall into the habit of eating practically all of the time. If we do munch and crunch day and night, we could end up with serious health problems later.

God created caterpillars to eat every minute. He expected people to control how much they eat.

"The good man eats to live, while the evil man lives to eat" (Prov. 13:25, TLB).

1. What do caterpillars eat?
2. What happens to the skin the caterpillar outgrows?
3. How can you improve your diet?

seven

Tough Dandelions

Every spring a massive army of determined homeowners march out to their lawns. Each soldier is armed with knives, hoes, lawn mowers, hoses, spray cans or bottles of chemicals. The time has arrived again to do battle against the enemy.

At first glance the invaders look innocent. They stand only a few inches high and have a yellow flower. But, despite their appearance, these soft buds with green pointed leaves are tough.

Homeowners will spend days hacking, spraying, cutting and hauling, hoping to eliminate the dandelion. Yet after so much widespread war, the dandelion only seems to have been defeated. In a few days, more yellow monsters will open their smiling faces. Next spring there may be as many dandelions or more returning to the same lawn.

Each year millions of people work hard and spend thousands of dollars to erase the dandelion. Some residents are successful, but not many. Dandelions are well and prosperous in most sections of the world. They get their names from a lion's tooth because of the jagged edges on their leaves.

You have probably seen neighbors get down on their knees and carefully cut off the top of each dandelion. Next year they will get a chance to hack them off again. Dandelions seem to love being chopped out. They will come back with more plants than were originally taken off.

Tired of the useless war, we could make peace with this weed by learning to use it. We could wear them in our hair. Possibly we should cook their leaves and include them for supper as people all over the world do. Some are made into beverages and even turned into medicines.

If you keep fighting dandelions you might win, but few people come out victoriously. Changing our attitude would probably be cheaper and less backbreaking.

Watching the dandelion hang in there under the toughest of circumstances must be an inspiration to all of us. They get knocked down, cut off, poisoned and hated, but they stand firm.

Christians do the same thing. Sometimes we are insulted, misunderstood, abused, neglected, disliked and even attacked. But the tough ones hang on. They believe that their faith in Jesus Christ is more important than any hardship. Christians keep coming through no matter what they suffer.

"When the storm has swept by, the wicked are gone, but the righteous stand firm forever" (Prov. 10:25).

1. How did the name dandelion originate?
2. If the top of a dandelion is cut off, will the plant die?
3. Have you observed a Christian who hung tough through a hard time? Tell about it.

eight

Amazing Facts

New Zealand has a gnat that glows in the dark. Called a fungus gnat, it lives in the Wartomo Cave. The larvae—not the adults—use the lights to attract other insects. Curious insects soon become part of the fast food menu.

Nine-banded armadillos can gulp air to inflate their bodies like footballs. They pump themselves up in order to float across rivers.

Tigers in the wild may eat 40 pounds of meat a day. How much does the average person eat?

Bugs live practically everywhere. The petroleum fly actually lays eggs in pools of black oil. Its eggs hatch into larvae that feed on other insects that get trapped in the oil. As the larvae get older, they burrow their way into the dirt next to the oil. There they safely turn into adult petroleum flies.

Kangaroos live only in Australia, but it is believed that they once hopped across Europe, South America and North America.

When a male avocet picks out a girlfriend, he first talks to her only by head movements. No sounds are exchanged—just plenty of nods, jerks and bounces.

The lowest form of animal is the microscopic amoeba. It has no legs, eyes or skeletal structure.

Starlings are birds that were brought to America to appear in Shakespearean plays. Those first 40 birds multiplied so rapidly that now in one single block in Washington, D.C., there may be as many as 10,000.

Flying squirrels have flat tails unlike their bushy tailed relatives. They use them to help guide their glide to the ground and serve as a brake.

These are amazing facts about God's creation. But do you know what is greater than all? That Jesus promised us life after death if we believe in Him.

"I am the resurrection and the life. He who believes in me will live, even though he dies; and whoever lives and believes in me will never die. Do you believe this?" (John 11:25).

1. How do nine-banded armadillos cross rivers?
2. Tell about the petroleum fly.
3. How does a flying squirrel use its tail?

nine

Noisy Shells

We brought a conch shell back from one of our trips. My wife, Pat, picked it up on the beach. We shined it ourselves instead of buying an expensive one in a shop.

Conch meat is a common food along the shores of Belize and throughout the islands of the Caribbean. The fisherman cuts out a piece of the shell in the back and is then able to pull the meat out easily. If he pulls slowly, the meat can be pulled out without breaking the back of the shell.

When I was a child people told me that if you hold the peach-colored shell to your ear, you can hear the ocean roaring inside. They said the shell had heard the ocean for so long that it would now hold the echo forever. With wide eyes I would hold a shell up and picture the bottom of the sea with all of its creatures swimming around.

Today I know better and I am a little sorry I do. If I put my two hands to my ear and cup them closely I can hear that same ocean sound. The reason I can hear a sound is that the air moving inside my hands sounds like ocean waves.

When I hold a conch shell next to my ear, it is the gentle moving air inside the shell that gives the sound. I still want to believe it is the ocean, but I know it isn't true.

Many things go on that we can't see and often can't explain. We see what the wind does or we hear the noise it creates, but we can't see the wind.

God's Spirit is like the wind inside the conch shell or the wind whistling in a canyon. We can't actually see the Holy Spirit, but we can see what He does. The Spirit changes people, guides them, comforts them, speaks to them—even silently. We don't see the Spirit moving from place to place, but He is still there.

Everyone who is born again and becomes a Christian has the Spirit of God working in his life. We don't see the Holy Spirit but He helps us anyway.

"The wind blows wherever it pleases. You hear its sound, but you cannot tell where it comes from or where it is going. So it is with everyone born of the Spirit" (John 3:8).

1. How do fishermen remove conch from the shell?
2. What causes the noise you hear when you put a conch shell to your ear?
3. What has the Holy Spirit done for you?

ten

When Animals Retire

Grandparents need to know what they will do when they retire. Where will they live and how will they stay active? A great many animals need to have a place to retire, too.

What happens when a family buys a pet lion cub because they believe it looks cute? When the lion grows up to weigh 300 pounds, it no longer fits in the house, it eats more than a human and is no longer cute.

Some animal lovers have opened retirement centers to help animals who need a place to go. They own several acres where these aging creatures can run freely and live out the rest of their days in peace.

Circus chimps whose performing days are over can run through fields, climb trees and be cared for. Baby zebras who were not wanted by the zoo where they were born are welcomed at these centers. Most families have no place to keep a rhino. It, too, would be welcomed at one of these places.

The operators of these centers would rather release the animals and let them enjoy the wild. The problem is that most animals would have little idea of how to survive. For years they have received food from trainers and keepers. A few have never spent one night in the rain. They have never hunted for food and are barely able to defend themselves in case of an attack.

Animal lovers all over the world have sacrificed their own money to care for these homeless creatures. Some have spent millions of dollars of their own wealth. Others have worked hard to raise money to support these centers. Those who are able sell the offspring to buyers who can furnish good environments.

Not everyone is cut out to care for a 500-pound Siberian Tiger. Love is the first ingredient a keeper needs plus the ability to hold a huge cat that suffers from a toothache at three o'clock in the morning.

Texans seem to have hearts almost as big as their state. Over 600 ranchers have adopted exotic pets that normally roam in Africa and Asia. The word "texotics" describes the exotic wildlife now being bred in that state.

Homes for wild animals may not be your thing. Not many of us want an orphaned giraffe living in our apartment. Our parents might complain about a 30-pound vulture in the dining room.

Yet it is important that we respect and care for animals. They're part of God's prized creation. And God gives high marks to anyone who treats them well.

"A righteous man cares for the needs of his animal" (Prov. 12:10).

1. Why can't pet animals be released in the wild when they are old?
2. What state has over 600 ranches that adopt exotic pets?
3. If you have a pet, how do you care for it?

eleven

Walking Trees

If ever there was a tree that liked to be of help, it must be the mangrove. These residents of the tropics not only provide housing for animals, but they also build up the environment by creating more land. When mangroves grow in the right places, they are friends to everyone.

This tree isn't hard to spot because you can see it taking a walk. It's no illusion. A mangrove stretches its long legs out into the water as it plants new seeds.

The trunk remains in the same place but the branches reach out and downward. A branch holds a seed which opens into a seedling. Mangroves must have salt water. When the branch dips beneath the water it finds the bottom, and soon the seedling catches hold in the mud. From there new legs begin to sprout.

By doing this the mangrove tree has formed legs, like spider legs, that arch across the water. Before long the branches turn into shopping centers for a large variety of creatures. At first things get trapped. Wood, cans and leaves become stuck. These are followed by tiny living creatures like snails or sponges.

Higher forms of life, like crabs, begin to shop there for food and houses. Raccoons might join the community to look for both food and shelter.

What began as a seedling on a branch, searching for a place to take hold, has now become a busy city. An assortment of birds moves into the area to enjoy the bustling activities.

There are several ways for a mangrove tree to sprout new trees, but walking out into the water is one of the most interesting. If the legs collect objects and silt, as is normal, it will create a new section of land. The area beneath its legs will build up above the water and a new patch of dry land will exist.

Unfortunately this dry land will probably mean the end of the original tree trunk. Salt water is needed to survive and the creation of more land places the trunk too far away. The mangrove tree puts itself out of business as it walks across the water.

Much of nature is destructive. Volcanoes, storms and tornadoes can each raise havoc on the world. But some of creation is known for the unique way it helps make our environment better.

People fall into the same categories. Some of us choose to tear things apart. At other times we follow the example of God. We look for ways to help, to build up, to make life go better for others. That's the attitude God has.

"God has come to help his people" (Luke 7:16).

1. Why are mangrove trees called walking trees?
2. How do mangrove trees improve the environment?
3. Name one good thing you will try to do today.

twelve

Lizard Push-Ups

Have you ever wondered why flies don't turn into ice cubes during the winter or why lizards don't become popsicles on cold days? Many small creatures *do* die when the thermometer takes a plunge. However, some survive even bitter cold because they have special ways of being protected.

Many insects, especially their larvae, live through the winter because they can change their water and fill up with anti-freeze. Just like our cars, these creatures need a liquid that will not freeze during cold weather. God has made it available.

Their tiny bodies can create a fluid called glycerol. It would take terribly low temperatures to make this liquid freeze. With the glycerol in place they look for a warm shelter to help them live through a tough winter.

People may have a similar fluid that their bodies could manufacture but we aren't exactly sure. We are used to putting on coats, turning up thermostats and piling on blankets. Our bodies aren't asked to fight extreme cold. Some scientists believe we carry more weight partly because our bodies don't use the fat to fight cold.

Snakes are good at using nature to warm them up. Early in the morning they will crawl out and stretch across the grass. They are allowing the sun to heat their skin. This action, called "basking" increases their body temperature by several degrees.

Other animals fight the cold by using exercise programs. Men and women can raise their temperatures merely by walking, jogging or chopping wood. Butterflies warm up by doing "arm rotations." Before it begins to fly, a butterfly will vibrate its wings to increase its temperature.

Lizards raise their heat with a workout. The little creatures hop up on a rock and start doing push-ups until they feel warm.

The system doesn't work for everyone and probably shouldn't. If every bug lived through the winter, in a few years we would be overrun with beetles and flies.

People have better systems than animals because our climate control is run by our brains. We can construct heating plants, design clothes, build houses and manufacture heating pads in ways that animals could never completely match.

God is in the protection business. He wants people to survive the extreme weather so we can enjoy life and serve Him. If He wanted to, God could change the temperature of the world a few degrees and wipe out a large number of us. Fortunately, His main job is protection, not destruction.

There are many ways we could have been hurt, destroyed or even frozen. But God works to help and protect us all of our lives.

"But let all who take refuge in you be glad; let them ever sing for joy. Spread your protection over them" (Ps. 5:11).

1. What fluid do insects use to survive the winter?
2. How do butterflies raise their body temperature?
3. How does God protect you?

thirteen

Turkeys Wear Out

Wild turkeys are back and growing in great numbers in the United States. That's good news because we had hunted so many that they almost disappeared. And if they disappear in America they will be *gone*, since this is the only place the turkey lives naturally in the wild.

Our Pilgrim fathers loved the bird and hunted it freely, but the turkey was too easy to catch. After hundreds of years many states made it illegal to shoot the bird, and its population began to increase again.

Most of the turkey we eat is of a different variety than the eager Pilgrims enjoyed. The store turkeys come from a group that originated in Mexico. Wild turkeys have a distinctive taste. Part of that comes from the food they eat in the woods.

Wild turkeys are built for short, fast flights. If they sense someone creeping up on them, they can burst into the air with almost no room to take off. Hitting directly in the air, the turkey can reach speeds of about 40 miles an hour almost immediately. That's remarkable since many birds of flight can't fly much faster.

If a turkey could keep up that speed, it would be amazing for a bird that lives on the ground. The problem is they can't keep it up. After carrying 25 pounds for a short distance, they have to land.

Part of the turkey's problem is its white meat. Birds that can fly long distances have more red pigment in their muscle. The red pigment and oxygen mix to give extra energy. Wild turkeys lack the extra punch.

Not that they are complaining. Turkeys seem more com-

fortable on the ground. They like to make a mad flight into a tree now and then but are basically content to stay earthbound. Even their nests are simple clearings in a bunch of dried leaves that they have shuffled around.

Though they need only short runways, the lack of ability to endure is a serious problem. If they could fly farther, more of them might live longer. Their quick burst into the air often makes them excellent targets for hunters.

Imagine for a minute that God's love came and went in short, rapid bursts. God would care about you a great deal today, but then He would get tired and stay away for a couple of weeks. He would be enthused, energetic and helpful for a few hours, but soon He would have to retreat for a long rest.

God is better than that. He stays around day after day. He doesn't tucker out, wear down, or take coffee breaks. Steady as a rock, God hangs in there every day.

"His love endures forever" (Ps. 106:1).

1. Describe a wild turkey's flight.
2. Describe a wild turkey's nest.
3. How would you tell a friend that God's love doesn't ever quit?

fourteen

Lovable Llamas

When you travel west on Interstate 80 in Nebraska, look carefully to the south. Along the highway a farmer keeps a half a dozen or more llamas. They are among the cutest and friendliest animals in nature.

Related to the camel, this hairy, long-necked creature has a slight grin and can wiggle one ear at a time. If it wants to, the llama can be difficult to get along with. It is a good pack animal but if it's overloaded, the owner has immediate trouble. The llama simply sits down wherever it is and goes on strike. Only after the burden is reduced will the beast agree to stand up.

They make excellent pickup trucks. Llamas stand around five feet at the shoulders and can haul equipment or supplies for 20 miles a day. In the United States some hikers use them for trips into the mountains.

It is believed that llamas do not fare well in the wilderness. Most of them throughout the world are owned and cared for by someone. Even the ones we see roaming about loose probably have a home on a ranch or a farm.

Normally we associate the llama with mountains, and they certainly are comfortable in the Andes. However, they function equally well at sea level and find Nebraska no serious hardship.

If a llama becomes angry, it gives off a few warning signs alerting everyone to back away. It will lay those high ears down against its head. And if the llama is especially upset, it knows how to spit like a camel.

No troublemaker, it would rather sunbathe or hum gently to its children as it feeds them.

Llamas are valued for their strong backs. They are also in demand for their milk, their hides and in some cases their good quality wool. This is especially true of their cousin, the alpaca.

Where did neat animals like this come from? How were they created or put together? We don't understand everything that went into creation or exactly what the process was. But we do know that God commanded that the llama come into existence and it did, because nature does what God tells it to do.

Birds that imitate frogs, turkeys that take off at 40 miles an hour, dolphins that talk and llamas that can wiggle one ear at a time—these were originally created by our God, who has plenty of imagination.

"Let them praise the name of the Lord, for he commanded and they were created" (Ps. 148:5).

1. If a farmer overloads a llama, what happens?
2. Name two ways llamas help people.
3. Name an unusual feature of an animal.

fifteen

Man-Sized Lizards

We didn't see these lizards when we were in Central America, but our friend told us about them. When he took a canoe trip down the river, he saw five-foot long iguanas, members of the reptile and lizard family. They sat along the side of the bank eating plants, a bit of fruit and maybe an occasional bird.

My wife and I hope to go back and see these creatures. They look like monsters from the midnight movie.

It wouldn't be polite to say iguanas are ugly. They probably find each other rather attractive. However, their photographs show the iguana to have a frightening appearance. Their outward skin is usually covered with a soft spine that runs from one end to the other.

If you move toward most iguanas, they will hurry to get away. They look like fighters but actually are peace-loving creatures. When people get close, iguanas drop into the water and try to disappear. At night they often hide among the rocks.

It would be fun to see such large animals that don't like to fight but enjoy the peaceful life. If something or someone wants to fight the iguanas, most of them will simply slide away and wait for the pest to leave.

However, not every iguana is shy and retiring. The Conolophus loves to charge anything it considers dangerous. It dines on plants and grasshoppers but isn't one to run from a good fight.

Black iguanas also live in Central America and reportedly have miserable dispositions. If they think you are going to attack them, they will try to bite you or knock you over with their long spiney tails. The black iguana is barely two feet long but it can create a lot of pain.

Often we have put too much emphasis on fighting. Quick to pound it out with practically anyone, we think it's tough and cool to battle.

The Bible has a different view. If possible we should avoid trouble, not look for it. Too many people are hurt, too many are afraid, too many are sorry. Whenever we possibly can, we need to live at peace with everyone.

"Live in peace with each other" (1 Thess. 5:13).

1. Are most iguanas fighters or are they peace lovers?
2. What do iguanas eat?
3. How do you know when to be at peace with someone and when to fight?

sixteen

Strange Facts

The Dodo was a bird that weighed 50 pounds. They lived on the island of Mauritius. None have been seen since 1681.

It may be that the frogmouth bird of Asia and Australia has insects fooled. Some scientists believe the bird merely sits still with its colorful mouth wide open. Insects think it is a flower and fly directly inside.

You could spend the rest of your life studying beetles. There are at least 28,000 species in North America alone.

A toad can throw its tongue out farther than its body length. Its tongue is sticky and excellent for snagging bugs.

Even animals have a tough time telling poisonous mushrooms from safe ones. If you see dead mice near a group of mushrooms, they probably made the wrong choice.

We all have seen pigeons, but what kind of pigeons? There are at least 550 different species and subspecies of pigeons in the world.

Some scientists believe that hyenas in Africa actually chew through metal cages in order to eat the bait set for leopards.

The Voyager 2 spacecraft shot toward the planet Uranus, traveling at 50 times the speed of a pistol bullet.

Not all creatures develop great hunting skills. Herons are clumsy at collecting mice, insects, crabs and other foods. Consequently, many herons die during their first year.

Since 1921 over 60 people have died trying to climb Mount Everest. The mountain is 29,028 feet high.

Elephants are the largest land mammals. The second largest are the white rhinos. Some elephants weigh 10,000 pounds or more.

Prairie dogs got their names because they wag their tails and give a quick barking sound.

Giraffes were once called camelopards because people thought they looked like tall camels with leopard spots.

The satin bower bird has a great love for the color blue. Males try to impress their female friends by bringing blue feathers, blue pebbles and blue berries.

Did you know that we can have a place with God forever if we invite Jesus Christ into our lives and believe in Him?

"For God so loved the world that he gave his one and only Son, that whoever believes in him shall not perish but have eternal life" (John 3:16).

1. What animal can break the metal of a trap?
2. Name the largest land mammal.
3. Can you say John 3:16 from memory?

seventeen

Horses in the House

What do most of us picture when someone mentions a small horse? We probably imagine a pony or a newborn colt. But there is a type of horse that, when it is full grown, is much smaller than any of these. It is called a miniature horse and will stand a little over two feet tall when it is as big as it's going to get.

When explorers came to the Americas, they found no horses here. So, in 1519, Cortez brought some in. They proved excellent for transportation, work, wars and in some cases even good eating.

Normally a horse is measured by how many hands high it is. A "hand" measurement is about four inches. Consequently, a 12-hands tall horse is 48 inches to the high point on its back at the base of its neck. Many of the miniature horses are four to eight hands high. You could put the small ones on your lap.

Miniature horses are called lilliputian horses. The name comes from an island in *Gulliver's Travels* where the people were supposed to be only six inches tall. The island's name was Lilliput.

Having a horse live in your house as a pet may seem like a great idea and a few people do keep them inside. However, some towns have laws against keeping horses inside a house. Also a number of horse breeders believe you cannot house-train a horse, even a miniature one. If they have bathroom problems in your house, your parents will probably move them outside very quickly.

God must have had fun creating animals. They come in such wide variety of amazing looks and different abilities. God allows us to train, rearrange them a little bit, and enjoy them. But basically they remain the outstanding products of God's lively imagination.

"God made the wild animals according to their kinds, the livestock according to their kinds, and all the creatures that move along the ground according to their kinds. And God saw that it was good" (Gen. 1:25).

1. What are miniature horses called?
2. How tall is a miniature horse?
3. What are some good ways you can use your imagination?

eighteen

Why Do Pandas Somersault?

If you have two kittens in your house, it's obvious that they like to play. Sometimes they wrestle roughly, but neither is out to hurt the other. They tussle, attack and even bite, but they seldom tear off fur. If you have ever seen two cats fight in your yard, you can tell it is much meaner than the way your pets behave with each other.

There is also a similar playfulness among squirrels. When they race after each other up trees and across lawns, it makes you want to join in.

Not all creatures like to play, but a large number spend considerable time tumbling, chasing, hiding, twisting and pushing with their friends. This recreation time has many terrific results.

When two bears in the wild begin "horsing around," they have no intention of injuring each other. If these mammoth creatures were to forcefully tear into each other, blood and even bones would soon start flying in every direction. Actually they are careful not to strike other bears with their sharp claws because they know how much damage they could do.

How many animals have we heard of that like to play? We think of the otter, monkey, chimpanzee, dolphin, ape and seal. Wolves, birds, lambs, rats, dogs and penguins are only a few of the species that love to frolic.

Animals don't normally tell us why they spend so much time playing, but a few observations could be made. For one thing, playing games is probably a fantastic way to learn how to hunt and defend themselves. Hours of crawling, stalking, lurching and surprising their friends and relatives evidently puts them in great shape for the tough world they face.

Another obvious reason for play is that it helps their personality adjustment. It appears that the meanest, cruelest, angriest animals in nature usually don't know how to play. They are too uptight to relax and have a good time. This may not be true of every animal, but it certainly proves correct for most.

It does make sense. If we are playing, we definitely are not fighting. Rather, we are busy getting along with our friends.

Some tests indicate that when monkeys are separated from other monkeys, their personalities turn sour. When they are later put in with monkeys, they are irritable, grouchy, fearful and nervous.

The sounds of children at play make all of us feel better. It's a sign that things are going well. The same can be said of adults. When they are having a good time together, everyone gets along better.

The Bible uses the idea of children at play as a sure sign that life is going well. When God promised the Jews that Jerusalem would be a happy, peaceful place again, He said children would play in the city streets.

Play isn't just foolishness. God gave it to us to help keep us calm and happy. When we play the right amount, we all get along much better.

"The city streets will be filled with boys and girls playing there" (Zech. 8:5).

1. What is the advantage of animal play?
2. Name some animals that like to play.
3. How do you play together in your family?

nineteen

A Blue Jay's Reputation

Do you ever see blue jays hopping around in your backyard? If you live in southern Canada or in the United States east of the Rocky Mountains, you probably have a few close by. The blue jay with its pretty feathers and peaked hat will stay with you through the winter. They don't migrate but rather collect food so they can survive even in the snow.

We have a feeder in our backyard outside our kitchen window. We have fun watching the activity. The blue jays perch in our cedar tree. Unfortunately our cats, Bart and Jeff, look at the blue jays as a free lunch. Between the scurrying squirrels, the stalking cats and sprinting birds, our yard sometimes turns into a battlefield.

The blue jays are a welcomed sight, but their reputation could be better. On the one hand they make nature flourish and grow. But, at the same time, they have a reputation as destroyers.

One of their best contributions to nature comes from their ability to carry seeds and plant them. The noisy bird is a member of the crow family and likes to pick acorns out of the oak tree or nuts from other trees. They will then haul their food to a safe place and bury it for a meal later on. During the cold winter the blue jay will return and feast.

Moving nuts all day takes a great deal of energy. The birds might be storing them two miles or more away. Between the number of nuts they stock in the ground and the number they eat to keep flying, the blue jay needs thousands of nuts.

To save himself any unnecessary work, the blue jay checks out the nut before flying away. He rattles the nut in his bill to see if it sounds good. If the nuts don't measure up, he drops them to the ground immediately.

Fortunately for nature, the blue jay can't remember where he hides all the nuts. These nuts that are left then often germinate and produce new trees.

That is the part of the blue jay's reputation most of us like. The other side may be important, but it seems ugly.

To add to their diets, blue jays will raid the nests of other birds and eat their eggs. Sometimes they even eat young chicks. Creatures in nature eat each other all the time, but it still sounds like a terrible thing to do.

Our good reputations are worth having. We work hard and are glad that people realize how kind we can be. But when we mess up or do something awful, we begin to create a bad reputation. Bad reputations are hard to erase. It's much easier to get a good one and keep it.

"Or he who hears it may shame you and you will never lose your bad reputation" (Prov. 25:10).

1. Have you seen a blue jay?
2. Tell about blue jays burying nuts.
3. What is a "reputation"?

twenty

High Priced Mink

Why aren't there any mink in Arizona? Does anybody know the answer? Scientists tell us that mink live throughout Canada and the continental United States except for the one area. They are so hardy that they can live under practically any conditions, wet or dry. But they don't seem to like Arizona.

Mink pelts, or furs, are valuable because some ladies enjoy mink coats. It takes a great many pelts to make a single coat, which explains why the finished garment is quite expensive. The pelts most often used come from mink ranches. At last count there were 1,200 such businesses in the United States.

Trappers collect the small animals, but outdoorsmen don't think the numbers are dropping. The greater threat is home building. When people move close or change the wilderness, the mink is pushed around.

Mink are not picky about where they live. If necessary, they are comfortable in the water and like to dine on fish and crayfish. On dry land they go after a slew of mice, insects, waterfowl and muskrats. Occasionally they will raid a farmyard and do considerable damage.

One of the reasons why mink have a terrible reputation is their hunting and eating habits. They seem to kill far more than they are able to use for meals. This passion for destroying living things may be way out of control.

The mother takes her kits hunting—at first for insects and later for the big stuff. Adult mink are so swift they can sit by a stream bank and pull out trout. Trout are fast, and it's remarkable that a mink can yank them out of the water.

A second bad habit customary among mink is their miserable temper. For some reason almost all of them appear to be ticked off whenever they are around people. At first it would seem that the wild mink is not used to human beings and naturally will lunge at them. However, mink raised in captivity are equally irritable. Many mink keepers will say that when they put food in the cage of a mink, the animal would far rather go for the keeper's hand. They prefer attacking and ripping things apart.

Some of us know someone who is as hot-tempered as a mink. He gets angry easily, wants to throw things and tries to start fights. It makes us nervous to be around him.

It would be good if we could help him calm down. Maybe we could find out what makes him so upset. It would be good to pray for him. But if we can't help our hot-tempered friend, we might need to stay away from him.

People who keep exploding are sooner or later going to hurt themselves and those near them.

"Do not make friends with a hot-tempered man, do not associate with one easily angered" (Prov. 22:24).

1. How are mink pelts used?
2. Are mink swift? Tell about it.
3. Do you know someone who is hot-tempered?

twenty-one

Showing Off for the Girls

Even bats like to look good. And when a flying fox bat is around a female, he shows up in style. First he starts singing and flapping his wings simply to show off. Soon he adds to his beauty by displaying his long, white shoulder fur.

Normally the white shoulder fur is kept hidden in tiny shoulder patches. But they insist on looking their best for the ladies. When they flash their white shoulder fur, the girls know they are special.

When the flying fox bat isn't flirting with the females, he spends his time hunting for fruit or sleeping upside down. Not only does the flying fox bat have a vital purpose, it has several important functions in nature. Scientists argue that if they were removed, our plant life would be hurt.

There are two reasons why the flying fox bat is being hunted. The first one will surprise you, so tell your stomach to get ready. Many people like to eat bats. I don't know any good recipes for this delicacy, but some say it tastes good.

The second reason they are hunted is that they destroy fruit. Naturally those who want to protect the flying fox bat disagree. They argue that this bat is essential to good plant and tree life.

An active flying fox bat carries pollination from flower to flower. It transports fruit seeds by eating the fruit. The huge baobab tree needs this bat to help it pollinate. Figs, breadfruit and bananas are only a few of the fruit trees that need the services of this nighttime roamer.

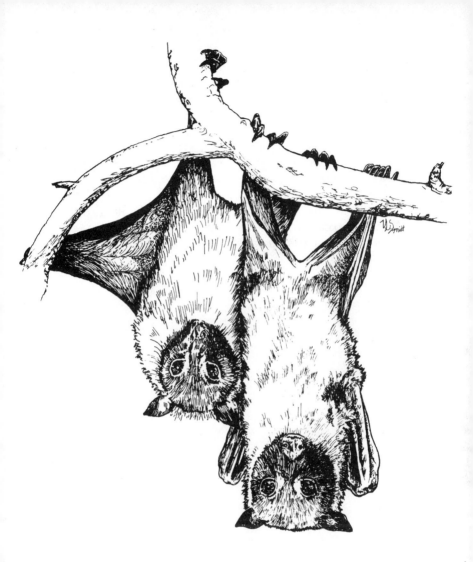

Among their own kind this bat does not lack for company. They hang from tree limbs all day in groups of possibly 150. Others wait in caves for the daylight to go away. When a mother flies, she often carries a young bat tightly against her stomach.

There aren't many people who are ready to believe that bats can do anything good. They don't want to know the truth because they are too busy being afraid of bats. Some people stay away from Christians for the same reasons. They think Christians are stuck-up and just sit around doing nothing.

The Bible tells us to prove our sincerity by doing good things—by helping others, by being kind, by sharing, by being thoughtful. If they see how we treat others, they will learn that our faith in God is real.

"Live such good lives among the pagans that, though they accuse you of doing wrong, they may see your good deeds and glorify God on the day he visits us" (1 Pet. 2:12).

1. When does a flying fox bat show its white shoulder fur?
2. Name one reason the bat is hunted.
3. How does the bat help in growing fruit?

twenty-two

The Strong Leopard

Leopards are large, beautiful, fast cats that have lived throughout Africa and Asia. Unfortunately, the huge hunter does not mix well with people and therefore has been reduced greatly in numbers.

In most areas it is illegal to hunt leopards for their fur. But since a finished leopard coat might sell in a store for $60,000, poachers still kill the animals and smuggle furs into other countries.

Leopard furs come in several colors. Most are basically tan with dark spots. However, they also come in white or black. Black leopards also have spots, but they are so dark it is hard to see them.

At one time leopards used to roam around the country of Israel. People in Bible times saw the colorful cats and often wrote about them. Leopards lived in Israel with lions, bears and wolves. That area was open to wildlife and was probably covered with a considerable amount of trees, bushes and jungle.

Much like the cats in our yards, the leopard enjoys climbing trees. It can perch on a limb and wait for supper to walk beneath the tree. Usually the meal consists of goat, sheep, snake, antelope or jackal. Once it has collected its food, the leopard again puts its tremendous strength to use. Grasping the prey in its teeth, the leopard will carry over 100 pounds up into a tree. There it will lay the carcass across a limb and keep it to chew on from time to time.

Because of the protection given by many governments, the number of leopards may be growing again. They need so much territory to roam and hunt that it is still hard to keep them separated from people.

The coat of the leopard was given to it for more than beauty. It is also more than just a warm wrap on a cold night in the mountains. The mixture of light color and dark spots makes it difficult to see and protects it from potential enemies—like people.

Like modern man, the prophet Jeremiah was impressed with the gorgeous coat of the leopard. Thinking of the giant cat, Jeremiah asked, "Can a leopard change its spots?" Could a leopard rearrange its spots or drop off a few? Would it be able to stack its spots on top of each other? The answer is obvious. A leopard can't change its spots in any way.

And, Jeremiah said, neither can a person who is used to doing evil turn around and start doing good. That's another reason why we need Jesus Christ. He can forgive us for the things we do wrong. And He can help us do things that are right. We can't do it entirely by ourselves. Not any more than a leopard can change its spots.

"Can the Ethiopian change his skin or the leopard its spots? Neither can you do good who are accustomed to doing evil" (Jer. 13:23).

1. What does a leopard eat?
2. Describe a leopard's fur.
3. How can a person change from doing wrong to doing right?

twenty-three

The Dog Wears a Mask

A new breed of animal could be moving toward America. First seen in Asia, these animals have now crossed into Russia and over the past 60 years swept over Europe. Before long they could be brought across the ocean where many Americans might see them for the first time.

Called the raccoon dog, it wears a short, black mask similar to the raccoon. However, it isn't closely related. Raccoon dogs are more like foxes. Even if they do become plentiful in America, the raccoon dogs will be hard to find. They roam around at night and sleep during the day.

One of the strange features about these dogs is that they share a bathroom. It isn't really a room but they have a special place where they go. The area could be from one foot around up to as much as five feet. Early the children (called pups) are taught to go to that one place until they leave home to lead their own lives.

Home is nothing fancy. They don't create complicated dens like a fox does. Rather, they find an opening in some weeds or set up housekeeping inside a tree. If necessary they can live under garages or other buildings.

As with many animals the fathers play a large role in helping to care for the young. They collect food for their families and spend a great deal of time grooming the pups. Each pup will grow to almost 2 feet long, not counting a 6-inch tail. Most have chunky bodies and weigh around 18 pounds when they are full grown.

Part of the reason why raccoon dogs are growing in numbers is their appetite for a wide variety of foods. They love a good meal of seafood, including fish or crab. The next day they might dine on fresh bugs or a small bird. They especially like fruit, berries or a side order of acorns. When seasons change they simply switch diets and still find plenty of food.

Despite the fact that raccoon dogs are hunted for their furs, the animal continues to increase in numbers. Even in areas where cities are being built and expanded, raccoon dogs can be seen in trees or roaming down alleys in the dark. The raccoon dog may not be extra bright like the real raccoon or the fox, but it is smart enough to change with its surroundings. When the weather changes or the streets become paved or trees are cut down, the raccoon dog merely finds a new way to keep going.

Sometimes all of us have to learn to change. If we keep doing things the same way, we could end up in trouble. If we have been taking things from our parents, we have to change and stop it. If we like to start fights, we soon have to quit that. If we are in the habit of telling little lies, we have to give them up.

God is pleased to see us change. He is the one who helps us change—we can't do it on our own. Both children and adults need to improve their way of living so that we treat each other better and live at peace with God.

"I tell you the truth, unless you change and become like little children, you will never enter the kingdom of heaven" (Matt. 18:3).

1. Describe the home of a raccoon dog.
2. What do raccoon dogs eat?
3. A raccoon dog knows how to change when it needs to. What can we learn from this?

twenty-four

Dump Truck Ants

My wife, Pat, and I rode in a four-wheel drive Landrover across rough roads with deep ruts and mud holes. We were on our way to Pine Ridge in beautiful Belize. It was our first visit to the Central American country located just beneath Mexico on the Caribbean Sea.

Our guide, Peter, knew the area well and had no trouble finding a large anthill six to eight feet wide. Trails of ants were coming from about four directions in straight lines. There were thousands of ants, each carrying a small leaf two or three times its own size.

Racing up and down along each line was a larger ant which acted like the boss. It didn't have a leaf but seemed to be busy keeping the other ants in line.

They hustled along. Not exactly running, it looked more like a rapid walk. There was plenty of motion—ants bobbing up and down as they hurried along. The boss ants scurried up the line and then back again as if they were giving silent orders.

The ants were hauling leaves into the gigantic mound and storing them in piles we couldn't see. When the supply was completed, the leaves would be allowed to rot or decompose. Later this would be food.

"Watch this," Peter said. He took a stick, placed it in one of the entrances and rattled it around.

"Better stand back," he added. "The guard ants will be out."

In about 30 seconds 20–25 huge ants appeared. They were so large their bodies twisted as they walked. Each ant was wide

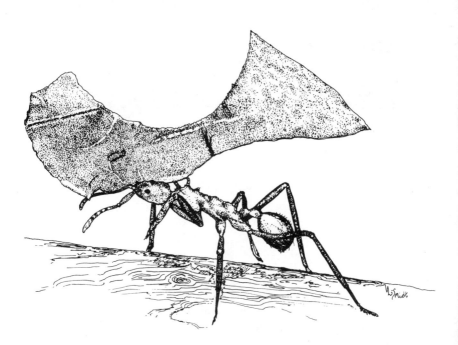

and black and built like a dump truck.

"If they bite you, it will sting like a wasp. They come out to attack beetles or whatever else might try to invade them."

The guard ants (or dump trucks) raced in every direction for a minute or slightly more. Finding nothing, they retreated inside. Meanwhile the working ants kept up their quick pace of carrying leaves.

Guards are an excellent idea for all of us. If we don't stay alert and be careful, we can easily end up getting hurt. One of the things God tells us to guard is our tongue. It's easy to say things that could hurt us and our friends.

Christians are careful about what they say. When we begin to repeat a rumor or say something mean, we hurry to catch ourselves. We serve God by controlling our words.

The next time we start to say something ugly, we ought to picture those dump truck ants. They are hustling to stop anything terrible from happening.

"He who guards his mouth and his tongue keeps himself from calamity" (Prov. 21:23).

1. Why do ants collect leaves?
2. Explain "guards for our mouths."

twenty-five

Leaping Snakes

Our guide used his machete to cut a path through the thick, clinging jungle. The large branches, leaves and vines hung over us, making it difficult for the sun to break through. Our feet could barely find places to step without landing on broken trees and flattened plants.

The short walk was far different from a hike in the forest. We couldn't see very far and the leaves and vines almost smothered us.

In the jungles of Belize there is an abundance of animals, including jaguars, monkeys, snakes and peccarries (similar to a pig). However, for the average person they are hard to find. Many of the animals would rather roam at night. They are not anxious to meet people. Animals are usually more afraid of us than we are of them. They hide in the dense jungle and normally are not seen by people unless they want people to see them.

In order for a healthy jungle to survive, it must have a rich soil to support it. Also jungles receive a high amount of rain every year. These two factors mixed with a generous amount of heat create nearly ideal growing conditions. This environment discourages too many people from living there and allows the flora (plant life) to reach enormous sizes.

The local people in Belize told me about a man who was working in the jungle where the leaping snakes live. This leaping viper with fangs sharp as razors carries a poisonous venom. If a person is bitten by this snake, he will need immediate medical attention. The leaping viper received its name because it can dart through the air the same distance as its length. Since it is three feet long it can leap one yard.

As the man worked, a leaping viper lunged at him and bit the man through his boot. He was quickly put in a Landrover and hurried to the capital city of Belmopan. He survived after receiving medicine to resist the poison.

Most snakes are not poisonous and are certainly unlikely to attack a person. However, we have to be careful in unfamiliar areas.

It always makes sense to be careful. When we begin doing foolish things, we easily get hurt. People who disobey God's law are just like those who walk among snakes—they find out it's easy to be hurt.

Careful people learn God's laws and obey them. Those who don't may end up in more trouble than they want.

"But be very careful to keep the commandment and the law that Moses the servant of the Lord gave you" (Josh. 22:5).

1. Describe a jungle.
2. Describe a leaping viper.
3. How do God's laws help us?

twenty-six

A Central American Cave

In the nation of Belize we explored a high-ceilinged cave few people get to see. It is located in the mountains, near a 1,000-foot waterfall. Most tourists don't know it exists. Even the local Indians and nationals seldom travel to this area.

We had to climb down a slippery bank to see the opening to this cathedral size cave. Long vines hung across the mouth making it difficult to see inside.

The cave wasn't long. From the entrance we could see the sun shining in from the other side. It had plenty of light so, once past the vine, we didn't need lanterns.

At the bottom of the cave was a sandy area where our friend had spent nights camping alone. Next to the sand was a beautiful pool that had been muddied by the recent rains. Normally this water would have been clear.

On the far side of the cave was an amazing stairway. Made of limestone the steps were almost perfectly shaped. They looked like men had carefully carved the steps in hopes that tourists would travel here. However, that is not the case. Over the years the many water levels in the cave have eaten away at the limestone. The water levels have formed at such even depths as to create a nearly perfect set of steps by nature's own hand.

The ceiling of the cave was too high and dark to allow us to see if any bats or other creatures had made homes there. If we had had flashlights and more time, we would have liked to explore it further.

As we stood in the cool, damp cave a sense of awe overcame us. Its size, beauty, and even its mystery made us feel that we had found a special place. In unusual, gorgeous places like this, we sense the fact that God is everywhere. He does not live only on top of the earth or high above the clouds. God is found beneath the ground, living where few people ever travel.

God is everywhere we go. He leaves His marks for us to see. No matter where we go or what we do, God will be present and will give signs of His presence if we are looking for them.

"In his hand are the depths of the earth" (Ps. 95:4).

1. Describe the floor of a cave.
2. Does it make you feel good to know God is everywhere? Tell about it.

twenty-seven

Kakapo Paradise

In the dark nights of New Zealand you can still hear the booming sound of the kakapo parrot. Its call rolls across a valley and can be heard for half a mile. For many years this two-foot-long bird lived in its own paradise, enjoying life at a leisurely pace, afraid of little or nothing.

The kakapo grows wings that are of practically no use. Kakapoes don't fly but rather poke slowly around the mountains in search of berries and seeds. Their idea of a special treat is to munch on a lizard.

There has never been any reason for them to hurry. A kakapo can live for 50 years if nothing bothers it. They take their good time at having chicks. Usually they reproduce only once or twice every ten years.

Kakapoes even look content. They weigh a pudgy six pounds, look like feathered penguins and walk like a happy duck. People don't see them often, but recently they have been photographed doing their famous booming call.

The good life for the kakapo probably could have continued if they hadn't been invaded. It apparently had no enemies— until human beings arrived 1,000 years ago. People brought dogs and rats with them. Soon the defenseless kakapo became a source of food.

Before long, man began cutting down trees and the kakapo found fewer places to live. People had to have places to live and so did birds, but it looked as if there was no room for this parrot. The number of kakapoes dropped so low that only 30 were believed to exist in the world.

Scientists became organized and tried to discover ways that

both people and kakapoes could survive. They began to hold back the enemies of the parrot.

Kakapoes make excellent pets; however, they don't seem to want to have chicks while in captivity. Consequently, scientists are trying to set aside areas where the kakapo can live in the wild and be protected from enemies. There are now possibly 100 in the world and their numbers could grow. Unable to fight back, this parrot's best hope rests in people who really care for it.

None of us lives in a paradise where there are no enemies. There are people who want to sell us drugs. We often meet someone who wants us to steal. There are many invitations to try alcohol—and then to try some more.

These people act like our friends but really they are enemies. If we say yes we could end up hurt or in trouble.

We have an offer from God. If we are willing to resist our enemies, He will help us fight them off. It may not be easy, but it can be done. We don't have to do it alone because God will give us strength and courage.

"With God we will gain the victory, and he will trample down our enemies" (Ps. 60:12).

1. Can kakapoes fly?
2. Why is the kakapo in danger of extinction?
3. Who are people enemies?

twenty-eight

The Sea Lion Trap

If you have ever gone to a sea animal show, you may have watched a talented sea lion perform. It can learn to bounce a ball on its nose, throw balls back and forth with other lions and even jump out of the water and sit on a box. If you live in southern California, you may have seen them in the wild playing in the water or sunning on the rocks.

Part of the reason why sea lions are fun to train is that they have a natural curiosity. They want to try new things and investigate new places. That same curiosity sometimes gets them into deadly trouble.

Five species of sea lions live in the world. One of the lesser known is the Hooker sea lion that lives south of New Zealand. Based on the Campbell and Auckland islands, they led fairly peaceful lives until man and rabbits invaded their territory.

When explorers discovered the sea lions in the early 1800s, the animals were so numerous that they barely fit on the islands. Sea lions snuggled together and sunned side by side. Word soon spread that sea lions were plentiful and ships from several countries raced there. They slaughtered fur seals and sea lions so drastically that the population almost disappeared in just 25 years.

Hunters stopped coming for the next 30 years and the sea lions lived in peace again. Their numbers increased and before long the islands were covered with 800-pound sea lions. However, by 1865 the word was out that the lions were back. During the next 15 years more boats came and the sea lions were slaughtered.

Finally, the New Zealand government stepped in and began protecting the sea lion.

Government action kept the sea lions safe from man, but that didn't erase the problem of rabbits. Over one hundred years ago the French introduced the feral rabbit to the area. Rabbits do not look as though they could hurt a sea lion, and they don't do it intentionally. However, thousands of sea lions die in rabbit burrows or homes.

The rabbit builds a home in the ground so it can raise its family. When a sea lion pup sees the home in the ground, its curiosity rises. It begins to nudge at the opening and check it out. Two or three pups force their way into the rabbit burrow and become stuck. Unable to turn around, they die from lack of air.

It would be nice if signs warned sea lion pups to stay out. It would also be good if their parents could teach the pups the danger. But many of them have to find out for themselves.

People are curious like sea lions. Curiosity is a great gift

that no one wants to lose. However, we also need to be careful so we don't get hurt or hurt someone else. That's why God gave us laws—not to be mean, but to help and warn us so we won't get hurt. People who ignore God's instruction are moving toward trouble.

"Hear, O Israel, and be careful to obey so that it may go well with you" (Deut. 6:3).

1. Name one reason sea lions can be trained.
2. How is the rabbit dangerous to a sea lion?
3. Do you know someone who is so curious that he goes too far and gets into trouble?

twenty-nine

The Zoo in Your Library

Don't look now but there could be a host of tiny creatures living in your local library. If you listen carefully, you might even be able to hear them. Some of the noises you hear are creaking wood, but probably not all of them. There may also be small insects making munching noises as they eat.

We call people who read a great deal "bookworms." Bookworms do exist, and they are chewing their way through many libraries.

What does a bookworm consider good eating? That depends on the insect. The spider beetle enjoys gnawing straight through a book. They have been known to chew their way through a line of 25 books or more.

Other varieties love paper or book glue. Some make a feast of the fungus on the books or the food that sometimes is left by busy readers. For special treats they eat the algae or pollen or mold that books might collect.

Well-lighted libraries with plenty of fresh air have fewer bookworms. The insects look for dark corners with high humidity or dampness. If no one checks out the book for a year or more, the worms (or lice, as they are sometimes called) eat away undisturbed.

Frequently, these destructive monsters are deposited in books as eggs. Later they hatch and, as larvae, begin to eat their way from volume to volume. They are just as much a problem in museums and maybe more destructive. Making their way into cases and displays, they eat delicate parts of exhibits. You may find the legs or the eyes of creatures on display missing. This probably means the "booklice" have attacked the museum and are eating their way from showcase to showcase.

Don't use the threat of bookworms as an excuse to give up doing your homework. They aren't very harmful to people. Their numbers could be reduced remarkably if we would clean our bookshelves, keep the area dry and well-lighted and read our books more often.

There is one special book that neither worms nor lice are able to eat or destroy. It's called the "Book of Life." We don't know much about it except the Bible says that the names of Christians are written in it. When you ask Jesus Christ to come into your life, your name is recorded. That record is kept forever.

If you aren't sure about having your name in that book, you can invite Christ into your life and become part of God's family. The "Book of Life" is a family record of the believers who belong to Jesus Christ.

"Yes, and I ask you, loyal yokefellow, help these women who have contended at my side in the cause of the gospel, along with Clement and the rest of my fellow workers, whose names are in the book of life" (Phil. 4:3).

1. How do bookworms do damage in libraries?
2. How can bookworms be prevented?
3. What book can't worms and lice destroy?

thirty

Causing Landslides

Squirrels are among God's cutest creatures. You can see them running across telephone wires or sitting on the lawn chewing acorns. They bounce across the yard with their rust-colored tails bobbing up and down.

However, a few squirrels, especially ground squirrels, are not loved everywhere. Ground squirrels don't live in trees but in burrows dug beneath the ground. Normally they make their homes in the desert, on rolling meadows or on flat prairies. But some dig their homes on the sides of mountains and this is when people get especially angry.

Ground squirrels look cute and harmless. Their appearance is more like a chipmunk or a prairie dog. They come in red, brown, black, gray or even white.

Unfortunately, they enjoy large families and are willing to dig wide homes for their many children. A ground squirrel can birth four to twelve young each spring.

As the ground squirrel population rapidly increases, they make their colonies larger until they have dug up much of a mountainside. If a hard rain hits the loose dirt, a landslide can quickly result. When people have built large, expensive homes on those mountainsides, the results can be terrible.

California has a particular problem with hillsides and ground squirrels. During rainstorms $500,000 homes slide down the hills. If squirrels had not dug homes in these areas, the destruction may not have occurred.

When 500 squirrels take up residence in one area, the ground can become soft. Squirrels can weaken dams and threaten the homes of hundreds of people.

This creates a problem. People don't want to get rid of the squirrels, but they cannot permit the destruction to continue.

The squirrels don't know any better. They don't want to see their burrows or homes washed away either. But even if they fail to understand the destruction they are doing, they still must be stopped.

When people refuse to be careful, we can do a great deal of harm, too. If we lie or steal or cheat, we hurt others as well as ourselves. Before we realize what we have done, we have created more problems than we can correct.

We all need to watch what we do. Christians don't want to bring pain to themselves or to others.

"But one sinner destroys much good" (Eccles. 9:18).

1. How does a ground squirrel do damage?
2. Do you know a person who hurts other people? Tell about it.

thirty-one

Unusual Facts

Did you know that the praying mantis has only one ear? It is located in the center of the creature's back. Researchers used to believe the mantis was deaf, but they now think it can hear sounds far out of our human range.

Terrible stories have been told of tigers attacking people in India. Over a period of time a tiger in Champawat killed 436 humans. Some authorities believe that mainly wounded tigers kill people.

Large birds may have as many as 25,000 feathers.

A trained pigeon can travel halfway across the United States and still find its way back home.

Pelicans have a different way of feeding their young. The mother swallows a fish and allows it to partially digest in her stomach. She then brings the food back up into her pouch-beak and allows her young to eat from it.

It is believed that no two zebras are striped exactly alike. Each has its own pattern like a human's fingerprints.

In order to keep its 12-ton body healthy, a sperm whale eats 800 pounds of fish a day.

When a peregrine falcon soars down to grab a small bird, it can reach a speed of 250 miles per hour.

A baby Emperor penguin can sit on its mother's foot and get a free ride around the territory.

The Bittern bird is a ventriloquist. Scientists believe it can "throw" its voice to fool attackers.

Centipedes have as many as 173 pairs of legs. The first pair of legs are poisonous claws. The poison is strong enough to make human beings sick.

Each of us can know God by believing in His Son, Jesus Christ.

"Jesus answered, I am the way and the truth and the life. No one comes to the Father except through me" (John 14:6).

1. How may feathers does a large bird have? 4,000 25,000 100,000?
2. How does a pelican feed its young?
3. How does a baby Emperor penguin get a free ride?

thirty-two

Hiding in the Rocks

Have you ever seen a small, mouse-like creature spreading leaves on a rock? If you have, it was probably a pika drying its "hay" before storing it for the winter. This six-inch rock-dweller has enough sense to get ready for the long cold months that lie ahead.

Pikas don't hibernate and often their homes are covered with snow. If they don't store enough to eat, they could starve before spring.

The pika collects plants for its pantry. To stay healthy they have to eat large amounts, which means the haystacks will need to be sizable. A pika will mark off its territory beneath the rocks or boulders and stuff that area with food.

Pikas can be found in many parts of the world. In the United States they are located in the Colorado Rockies and other mountainous regions. Scientists love to argue over how these creatures entered this country and whether they belong to the rodent or rabbit family.

Because of its size the pika needs clever ways to protect itself. Basically it is dependent on two forms of warnings: noisy and silent. If a pika sees a hawk flying near, it gives a terrible barking sound. However, if a ground animal enters its territory, silence is the better plan. Weasels will hear the barking and slide between the rocks to hunt the pika.

No matter who the attacker, the pikas' best hope of escape is to scurry between the rocks. They aren't large enough to fight back and must depend on a good hiding place.

They have relatives called coneys, or rock hyraxes, which have lived in Syria and Israel. Both Solomon and Jesus were probably familiar with these animals and watched them hustling among the rocks. They have quick feet that adapt easily to the hard surfaces they live on. Some have padded feet with small suction cups which help them climb in different situations.

Proverbs tells us that coneys, the pika-like relative, are creatures with little power. That is why they live among the crags of rocks (Prov. 30:26). The rocks protect them when they can't defend themselves.

There are many times when we are like the pika or the coney. We can't take care of ourselves. Maybe there are evil people who want to trick us and get us to follow them. Maybe we can feel ourselves being drawn to do something terrible and we don't know if we can resist it.

That's a good time to head directly for the Rock. Our Rock is God and He offers us protection. God, our Rock, will always provide us with a welcomed place when we need Him.

"The Lord is my rock, my fortress and my deliverer; my God is my rock, in whom I take refuge" (Ps. 18:2).

1. How does a pika store its winter food supply?
2. How does a pika protect itself?
3. Have you ever needed to find protection in the Rock? Tell about it.

thirty-three

Living Dragons

The San Diego Zoo recently tried to raise komodo dragons, but the experiment fizzled. Both the male and female died without leaving any babies. This was terribly disappointing to scientists since the number of dragons has been reduced to a few thousand and continues to dwindle.

Komodos are actually lizards but they are ugly enough and mean enough to be called dragons. Normally they are found on Komodo Island, an Indonesian territory only two-hundred fifty miles from Australia. No small creature, they can reach lengths of ten to twelve feet.

When angry, the komodo puts on a terrifying display. It rears back, thrusts out its tongue and makes a terrifying hiss. Its armor-looking scales and swinging tail are enough to make you wish a knight was there to rescue you.

It isn't just their appearance that makes people tremble. Komodos are extremely dangerous. They will kill a pig or even a water buffalo. Those who live among the dragons insist that dragons have killed and eaten people.

They may be exciting to study, but they don't sound like great pets. Having a komodo eat in your house could be more than your parents could handle. Watching a 365-pound dragon eat could be disgusting.

Not picky eaters, they will with one bite tear out the entire side of a dead animal. They gobble down bugs, fur, bones, whatever they manage to rip loose with the flesh. They would think nothing of finishing off an entire goat in one meal. Satisfied, the komodo would then probably crawl up on your couch and sleep for a week or more while the food settles.

Too bad their parents didn't teach them to control their eating habits. Dragons crunch, tear and smack at their food. If the selection doesn't agree with them, the komodos will simply throw up.

We are careful what we eat and how much. The habits we develop while we are young will help keep us healthy as we grow.

"If you find honey, eat just enough—too much of it, and you will vomit" (Prov. 25:16).

1. Are komodo dragons dangerous?
2. Are komodos really dragons?
3. Think of a way to make your eating patterns more healthful.

thirty-four

The Show-Off Frigatebirds

How many times have we watched someone showing off? Maybe it was a boy balancing himself on a fence or a girl dressing to look older than she is. Once in a while all of us do it. Even adults like to show off their cars or impress people with how much they know.

Nature is filled with creatures that like to do things to get attention. One of the most famous is the frigatebird. This bird lives in warm climates, looks graceful hovering in the sky and has a strong seafood diet.

The frigatebirds look almost motionless as they float in the air. Like kites, they wait over an area until they see a fish near the surface and then they drop down quickly. Sometimes they aren't too particular where they get their food and will steal the fish that other birds catch.

Frigatebirds can be fairly large. They grow to three and one-half feet long and may have a wing span of eight feet.

When a male frigatebird wants to show off for the females, he uses a balloon system. There is a red, wrinkled pouch located on his throat. He has a method of sucking air into the balloon and for nearly half an hour he blows it up.

For some reason the girl frigatebirds think this is macho and pay more attention to the show-off. That only encourages him. He struts around with his burly chest, making sure everyone see it. If he feels someone still might miss it, Mr. Frigatebird flies around like a colorful blimp.

His show goes on for hours. Once he fills his balloon, the frigatebird makes a big deal out of it.

There isn't anything wrong with the frigatebird playing this game. It's part of the bird's natural lifestyle. That's the way God made them.

When it comes to people showing off, it's another story. Sometimes we go too far trying to impress each other. If we aren't careful we do extremely dumb things.

How many times have we tried to show off how much we know? We act like we're smart and try to put others down. It's as if we are saying, "Look at me; I'm better than you."

The Bible tells us to stop showing off our knowledge. It's all right to be smart, but it's wrong to make others feel bad when we show off.

If we want to show something to others, let us show them how much we can love. Let's help our friends, let's think of them first, let's be kind. We can give love to our parents instead of acting like know-it-alls. And they can give love back to us.

"Knowledge puffs up, but love builds up" (1 Cor. 8:1).

1. Explain the frigatebird's balloon system.
2. Name some good things to show others.

thirty-five

Tricky Little Creatures

Animals may not be as smart as people, but they are excellent at pretending and fooling each other. Every day is a struggle for food. They need to know how to get a meal without becoming one themselves. To accomplish that they often use every trick you can imagine.

The dead-leaf butterfly is a good example of the actor in full costume. They not only have the same color as an old leaf but they also have a similar ragged edge. When they fly, the dead-leaf butterflies twist their bodies to look like falling leaves.

Bombardier beetles have an unusual method of fighting their enemies. They can squirt a foul-smelling fluid which becomes a puff of smoke when it hits the air, giving them time to escape. A couple of shots and practically any creature will back away. They aren't trying to fool anyone. The bombardier beetle really is dangerous.

There is another beetle, a relative of the bombardier. It is a tricky one. It will do a headstand just like the bombardier. Consequently, their enemies will beat a quick retreat, believing they might be zapped with smelly liquid. The pretending beetle then walks away with a grin on its face.

Have you ever stood by a tree and decided to lean against it? Were you surprised to see a piece of bark suddenly fly away? It looked like bark but was actually the underwing moth which sits around on tree trunks almost invisible.

Even the poor firefly has a rough life. Some of its bug relatives can imitate their flashing signals. If a firefly rushes over to answer the phony signal, it could immediately be eaten.

Scientists will continue to argue over how intelligent animals are. However, most agree that they are clever. An assassin bug is "smart" enough to use the carcass of a termite to draw other termites its way.

Animals are often born with some of their tricks and did not learn them. However, other forms of imitation may clearly be copied.

Trickery isn't confined to lower animal forms. Many people keep constantly busy trying to fool each other. They even brag about how they cheated someone or lied, as if deceiving a person is a talent they are proud of.

When we play games, it's fun to use tricks, but that isn't how we treat people in real life. We shouldn't try to deceive others and take advantage of them.

"Do not deceive one another" (Lev. 19:11).

1. How does a dead-leaf butterfly trick its enemies?
2. How does a bombardier beetle get away from its enemies?
3. Can you think of ways you will be honest and not try to fool others?

thirty-six

The Happy Acrobats

Why do gibbons carry their arms over their heads, wiggling them like loose spaghetti? Are they simply clowns looking for laughs from their friends? Gibbons aren't imitating baton twirling. The reason they carry their arms so high is they don't know what else to do with them.

This agile ape is more at home in the trees than strolling on the ground. A gibbon's arms are designed for climbing trees and not for walking. If they allowed their hands to hang down by their sides, as humans do, their knuckles would scrape the ground. They can also keep their balance better by twisting their arms as they hurry along.

If you want to see gifted gibbons at their best, watch them move among the trees. Normally they live in the high branches where they are as comfortable as any human in a living room. Gibbons don't need nests but prefer to sit on a branch far out from the trunk. When trouble comes their way, the little apes can shoot in any direction, racing from tree to tree.

Gibbons don't choose to fight their enemies unless they fight another gibbon. Their best form of defense is to race through the trees. They can run through the branches faster than you or I could run along the ground.

At full speed they can leap 25 to 35 feet in space from tree to tree. They are gifted acrobats with amazing hands. A gibbon hand does not have to grab a branch. Its hands serve more as hooks. They merely hit the branch and swing onto the next one.

Called brachiation, this movement greatly increases their speed.

Sailing in the air from tree to tree the quick gibbon can grab a bird while both are in mid-flight. He will then hit the next branch in almost perfect timing. If a gibbon needs to haul food to its family, it merely grasps the object in its feet and swings freely with its hands.

Those who work with gibbons believe they are highly intelligent as well as neat. They can be quickly taught to make their own beds and in some areas live with human families and their children. Some insist that the gibbon is merely another member of the household.

We all appreciate seeing talented animals. The gibbon can do a great many things I can't do. I don't carry food in my feet, and any attempts I would make to leap 30 feet from tree to tree could only get me hurt.

Fortunately, we don't need the same talents as these apes. Each of us has abilities and gifts. We aren't jealous of animals and we don't have to be jealous of other people.

We can be happy with the gifts God has given us. We learn to read, work computers, sing and tape programs on the video cassette recorder. God has given us so much ability we don't have to envy anyone.

Each of us is in God's gifted program because He has given all of us gifts.

"Every good and perfect gift is from above, coming down from the Father of the heavenly lights" (James 1:17).

1. Why do gibbons carry their arms over their heads when walking?
2. How are their hands used when gibbons swing from tree to tree?
3. Name five things you do well.

thirty-seven

Monkeys Need Monkeys

Why do we enjoy watching monkeys? Probably because they are a great deal like us. They almost stand up, they love to climb, and monkeys seem to have a thoroughly good time playing. No doubt they are fairly intelligent but not as smart as their ape relatives.

Not every monkey likes to frolic around in the trees. Generally speaking, we can divide monkeys into two basic categories: those that live in trees and those that move on the ground. The tree dwellers live in Central and South America. Ground monkeys are normally found in Africa and Asia. There are a few exceptions to these two categories and almost every monkey sleeps in trees. Some monkeys live different lifestyles but these are the ground rules.

Because of their separate living conditions they face different enemies. Red colobus monkeys in Africa live in savannas. These are low lying areas with few trees. They have to watch out for crocodiles and pythons. At the slightest indication of the danger, they shout warning calls and everyone scrambles.

Tree monkeys have a number of enemies such as jaguars, but they are also concerned with birds that fly in the sky. At any moment an eagle or similar bird could sweep out of the air and snatch a baby monkey. Living in the wild is extremely dangerous for either variety.

Danger is one of the reasons why monkeys live in groups. With two-hundred kinds of monkeys, most of them can still be

put into three types: the family groups, the many-male groups, and the single-male groups.

Marmosets, the smallest monkeys in the world (about the size of a mouse), are part of a family group, complete with one father and mother. The red colobus lives in a troop led by several males. Patas monkeys are headed by one male and his harem.

Monkeys are smart to live in groups because they need each other. When death occurs, they can adopt the children that survive. They spend many hours, up to six a day, grooming each other and picking off bugs. When predators approach, monkeys call out an alarm that sends all the monkeys to a safety zone.

If a monkey is threatened by a large cat, the other members of its group may come together. By forming a team they sometimes chase off a leopard or a cheetah.

Groups can be great. People need each other as much as monkeys and maybe more. Christians get together in churches, youth groups and Bible studies because people have a hard time making it alone.

We call this fellowship and it means we love and depend on each other. We encourage, teach, laugh, cry, listen and sing together because it's a bummer being alone. Our faith grows by sharing with Christians who are hanging together.

"We proclaim to you what we have seen and heard, so that you also may have fellowship with us. And our fellowship is with the Father and with his Son, Jesus Christ" (1 John 1:3).

1. Describe the three types of monkeys.
2. How do monkeys help each other?
3. How is your Christian group important to you?

thirty-eight

Saving Ferrets

Everyone thought the black-footed ferret was gone forever. No one had seen the animal in Wyoming for fifteen years despite continuous searching. Feelings of despair turned to happiness when a lady reported an animal that her dog had killed. They weren't happy because the dog had killed an animal but because maybe that was the ferret they were hoping for. And it was. Scientists identified it as the black-footed ferret, famous cousin of the weasel.

The search was on again in full force. Money was given by federal, state and private organizations to find and protect this wiry little creature. One researcher had spent over ten years looking for the ferret.

Most searches centered around prairie dog colonies. Black-footed ferrets like to move into a prairie dog's home, eat the occupants and live in the earth home. Unfortunately for scientists, ferrets like to stay inside for a couple of weeks, making them hard to spot.

Finally researchers began to sight ferrets. At Meeteetse they found nearly 40 living in 12 litters. Naturalists then took on the job of preserving the ferret and helping its population grow. This is where the Soviet Union became involved.

Practically every effort to get the ferret to breed in captivity failed. After enormous work and expense scientists wondered if the animal had any future. At this point the zoo in Moscow agreed to help by loaning six Siberian ferrets to the United States. They are the black-footed ferrets' closest relatives. Apparently their hope is to breed the Siberian ferrets with the black-footed ferrets and increase their population.

Why would scientists dedicate so much of their careers to saving this little known animal that practically no one has seen in the wild? Why would governments spend large sums of money? Why would nations agree to cooperate to save a rare animal that eats prairie dogs? All of this happens because people care what happens to even one of the minor animals in a huge world.

If they care this much for so few animals, imagine how much God cares for one person. He would do all of this and more to bring one of us to himself. God wants us to be part of His family. That's why He sent His Son to die on the cross. He considered one person, you, so important that God would sacrifice, suffer, search and work to get us to believe and serve Him.

Ferrets are valuable, but you and I are worth far more than any animal.

"Suppose one of you has a hundred sheep and loses one of them. Does he not leave the ninety-nine in the open country and go after the lost sheep until he finds it?" (Luke 15:4).

"I tell you that in the same way there is more rejoicing in

heaven over one sinner who repents than over ninety-nine righteous persons who do not need to repent" (Luke 15:7).

1. What kind of home does a ferret prefer?
2. How did the Soviet Union cooperate to protect ferrets?
3. How has God shown how valuable you are?

thirty-nine

Wapiti Is King

A lion may be king of the jungle, but the wapiti is king of North America and they have the crown to prove it. This majestic animal is an elk and a member of the deer family. If we aren't familiar with wapiti, we probably confuse them with the larger moose.

Their crown consists of a royal rack of antlers that the male grows every year. Antlers are different from horns in looks and build. Horns are hollow and can be used as trumpets, containers, and even hearing aids. Antlers are made of solid bone, are heavier and often larger. You never want to insult an elk by saying it has beautiful horns.

The adult wapiti, or white rumped elk, sheds its old antlers around March. Since he doesn't cast off both sides at once, he could be in an awkward fix for a time. Antlers are heavy, and if only one side is left the wapiti will have trouble keeping its balance. To correct the problem, the king will keep stabbing at trees and at the ground trying to dislodge the remaining half of its crown.

When the antlers are gone, he has four or five months to grow a new set. The place where the antlers grow is called a pedicel. Soon his body begins producing a new bone structure covered with a thin skin called velvet. When the antlers are grown he will rub this layer off.

The people who study antlers give each part a name. The stem coming out of the wapiti head is called a beam; the first branch of the beam is a brow tine, the second a bez tine, the third is a trez. All of the top branches are surroyals.

Occasionally a wapiti is seen carrying antlers with eight or more tines on each beam. It is considered a true monarch of the outdoors.

Why does a wapiti need antlers? Its main purpose is not self-defense. For most of their enemies a swift kick with their powerful hoofs is enough to send the enemy whimpering.

The big use of these antlers is to fight the other elk during mating season. Mostly it's for show. They don't usually do much harm to each other, but a mock battle is what all of the wapiti seem to expect.

Antlers are crowns to the male wapitis, and they look forward to them each year. God gives people crowns too, but they aren't always the kind you wear on your head. Each child is a crown for his grandparents. Like tine on an antler, children make the elderly and middle-aged feel like royalty.

When children spend time with their grandparents, they usually make them feel like kings and queens.

"Children's children are a crown to the aged" (Prov. 17:6).

1. How are horns and antlers different?
2. How often do wapiti get a new set of antlers?
3. What can you do this week to make your grandparents happy?

forty

Storks on Your Roof

How did the story start about storks bringing babies? No one can be certain, but it probably began in Europe. Storks made their nests on the roofs of homes in countries like Denmark, Holland and Germany. Because storks were considered good luck, they were welcomed. Some homeowners even built special platforms on their roofs to encourage the leggy birds to settle with them.

Legends were plentiful about the value of having storks live on your home. They were supposed to keep lightning from striking. Others felt their feathered friend brought financial prosperity. Thousands of storks lived in large cities, making the homeowners feel better.

While those stories were so popular, someone thought they noticed storks around houses just before a baby was born. Since they were near most houses most of the time, it was easy to believe stories about storks and babies being together. From that began the rumor that storks brought the soul to a newborn baby. How much people actually believed it is hard to say. Maybe it was simply an amusing tale.

It was a short jump from the idea of storks bringing souls to the myth that possibly they brought the entire baby. Later it was easier to tell the stork story than it was to tell children where babies really come from.

If the story isn't real, the stork is. They can be found in the United States, Asia, South America, Europe, Africa and Aus-

tralia. Storks look like they walk on stilts and reach a height of four feet. Despite their awkward appearance they can fly extremely well. Their landings look disjointed but they manage with reasonable safety.

Storks have an amazing ability to migrate thousands of miles. European storks fly to South Africa, making a round trip over 14,000 miles. While in Africa they live a different lifestyle, as if they were on vacation. Storks live along the rivers where they lead a rural life. They stay away from rooftop dwellings until they return to the cities of Europe.

As part of their normal route many storks travel across Israel. The prophet Jeremiah probably saw many of the gangly birds coming and going. He told us we could learn by watching the stork. Unable to read or write, yet the stork knows exactly what it is supposed to do and does it. Storks have enough sense to migrate when they need to because God created them that way.

You and I were created to obey God, but many of us fail to show the good judgment of a stork. We rebel, sin, disobey and throw tantrums. Too often we don't have the sense to follow God.

The next time we begin to do something foolish and disobey God, we should say to ourselves, "Even a stork is smart enough to keep God's laws."

"Even the stork in the sky knows her appointed seasons, and the dove, the swift and the thrush observe the time of their migration. But my people do not know the requirements of the Lord" (Jer. 8:7).

1. How did the story of storks bringing babies start?
2. Tell about the storks' migration.
3. How does a stork find its way when traveling?

forty-one

Adopted Monkeys

Have you ever seen a picture of an organ grinder on a street corner? As the man grinds, or cranks, the organ, his monkey on a chain dances around with a tin cup. When it approaches you, the monkey hopes you will throw a coin in the metal container. Better than a picture, maybe you have even seen the man and his monkey in person.

These little monkeys must be the cutest animals in the world. Most often they are the capuchin monkey. Found in Central and South America and the island of Trinidad, they live in small groups, traveling among the trees looking for food.

If you have ever eaten ice cream and found it smeared all over your face, you can imagine how some of these monkeys look after eating something. They eat and drink from flowers, and one of their favorites contains orange pollen. After drinking from these flowers, the baby capuchins usually have orange sprinkled over their faces. They look comical with their big round eyes and colored cheeks.

Jungles are dangerous places, especially for monkeys. They may have fun climbing trees and sampling exotic foods, but at any second they could be in life-threatening danger from eagles or large roaming cats. In one rapid sweep an eagle could scoop up a baby monkey and its life would be over.

Because of the hardships involved, many of the adult monkeys look out for the young. They help open hard fruit for them and stand guard while they eat it. If an adult tries to steal food, another adult will quickly come to the baby's rescue. When an eagle is sighted, a grown capuchin will begin issuing a warning call for the youngster to scurry for cover. The thoughtful adult will keep his siren going until the eagle has totally left the area.

Frequently a mother capuchin dies or is killed in the cruel jungle. Fortunately another mother will adopt the baby monkey and help guide it into adulthood.

There are a number of reasons why human children need to be adopted. Every year thousands of adult couples, who are waiting for a child to join them, adopt a boy or girl, or maybe more.

Every year millions of us at all ages are adopted into the family of God. We become His children by placing our faith in Jesus Christ. God doesn't want any of us to be spiritual orphans for any reason. He invites all of us to come to Him and let God be our Father.

"He predestined us to be adopted as his sons through Jesus Christ" (Eph. 1:5).

1. Where do capuchin monkeys live?
2. How do adult monkeys help young monkeys?
3. What do you think it means to be adopted into God's family?

forty-two

Did You Know?

Female kangaroos are called "flyers" because they travel so fast. Adult males are "boomers." Kangaroo children are "joeys."

Elephants are such good swimmers that they have been in the water for as long as six hours at a time.

Fur is really an extra thick growth of hair.

Cats walk on tiptoe. Their claws are hidden inside their paws but stick out in a second, ready for battle when danger is near.

Portuguese sailors thought coconuts looked like monkey faces. They named them coco which means monkey in Portuguese.

The lynx gets its name from its excellent eyesight. A wild cat, its name is Greek for "keen sight."

Turtles are the only reptiles that are toothless. Sharp beaks, however, can do any biting they may need.

The Irish elk is neither Irish nor an elk.

Ticks and chiggers are not insects but are members of the spider family.

A daddy longlegs has eight legs and belongs to the spider family. If a young one loses a leg, it may be able to grow a new one.

The Australian giant clam weighs up to 500 pounds.

Elephants are so careful they can crack a coconut shell without cracking the meat.

Unlike many of its cat relatives, the tiger seems to enjoy water. A mother tiger will take her cubs to a stream and teach them how to swim.

If elephants do not wear down their tusks, their front teeth will become too heavy to carry.

Reindeer have waterproof coats. The fur holds air and helps keep the animal up as it crosses rivers.

Did you know that Jesus Christ died for everyone and that includes you? He paid for our sins and prepared a place in heaven for us.

"But God demonstrates his own love for us in this: While we were still sinners, Christ died for us" (Rom. 5:8).

1. What are kangaroo children called?
2. What animal walks on tiptoe?
3. Which reptile is toothless?

forty-three

Deadly Tarantulas?

There aren't many words that send shivers up your spine, but the name tarantula probably gives you the chills. There are hundreds of scary stories about the hairy little spider with eight eyes. Once terrible tales spread, they are passed on for years, sometimes for centuries.

It's possible that a few people have died from the poison in a tarantula bite, but it can't be many. Tarantulas in South America could be dangerous, but normally a bite from one in the southern United States would only be as harmful as a bee sting.

Like most creatures, the tarantulas aren't eager to mix with people. Most of the time they hide around the entrances of their burrows, trying to avoid anything they can't eat. If they sense a stranger, the tarantula simply disappears. The idea of attacking a human being has probably never occurred to this spider.

The type of food they usually enjoy is a main course of grasshoppers or beetles. If they become large enough, their diet will include a juicy frog or lizard. One of their relatives is the bird spider of South America. With its legs extended, this tree dweller is larger than your hand and it attacks birds.

There are 30 kinds of tarantulas in the United States and six hundred varieties worldwide. The thousands of hairs on their bodies serve a double purpose. First, they seem to act as ears. The hairs pick up vibrations. Second, they become weapons. If an animal, like a skunk, sniffs around his burrow, the tarantula shakes off some hairs that get caught in the attacker's eyes and nose. They make the skunk so miserable it is happy to retreat quickly.

Despite the fairly harmless nature of the tarantula, its reputation as a killer has remained for hundreds of years. Movies have been made, stories written and told at campfires about the hairy-legged tarantula and its ability to kill. Most of the horrible details are imaginary.

Once a false story spreads, it's hard to erase it. That's why it's important not to start them. Too many people have been hurt for years because people were willing to believe a story that was absolutely untrue.

"Don't accuse people falsely" (Luke 3:14).

1. Are tarantulas in the United States poisonous?
2. What is the purpose of the thousands of hairs on their bodies?
3. How can you prevent false stories from spreading?

forty-four

Mini-Pigs

When we were visiting Central America, we heard that a member of a film crew had been bitten by a peccary. The man was taken to town and given shots to hold off the possibility of disease.

The animal that bit him was a small member of the pig family. Peccaries are only three feet long and stand a foot and a half at the shoulder. Pigs raised on farms are usually eight to ten times as large. Peccaries can be found in the state of New Mexico, Texas and Arizona as well as throughout the tropical countries.

Peccaries are highly sociable creatures that hang around in herds of 3 to 75. The hunter who goes after a peccary must be alert. Instinctively its friends and relatives will run to protect one of their own. They think nothing of attacking a person or animal who intends to hurt them.

A herd of peccaries mark off an area they want for their home ground. The territory may equal a total mile. Peccaries might look nearly all alike, but they have a way to distinguish each other. Special musk glands allow them to carry a distinctive odor. Members of their herd can tell from the smell who belongs to their group and they chase off the others.

When you get to know a peccary extra well, you can sit and check out its toes. For some reason they have four toes on the front feet and three toes on the hind feet. Possibly it gives them a firm stance while they root in the ground with their famous snouts.

It's hard to argue how intelligent a peccary might be. We have trouble explaining how intelligent people are. However, some evidence indicates a peccary can be taught to respond to its own name and no other.

Peccaries' real strength is the ability to establish a herd and maintain dependence on each other. They are stronger because of their numbers. They are more secure because they can count on each other in case of trouble. Food supplies are easier to keep because they do not allow other peccaries to steal from them.

Peccaries have developed a lifestyle designed to help each other. Christians do something similar. We meet together to encourage each other. If we have a need, we try to help each other. Christians also help those outside their group, but they regularly help other believers in Jesus Christ.

Christians don't make good lone wolves. We are more like peccaries who watch out for members of the herd.

"Be completely humble and gentle; be patient, bearing with one another in love. Make every effort to keep the unity of the Spirit through the bond of peace" (Eph. 4:2, 3).

1. Peccaries are members of what family?
2. Tell about peccaries' toes.
3. Tell how Christians you know help each other.

forty-five

Tents of Snow

Hunting in temperatures of 25 below zero can be dangerous if you don't know how to protect yourself. For hundreds of years the Eskimo or Inuit have known how to hunt seals in frozen conditions and yet stay warm at night when they sleep. When they need a warm place to bed down, they just build a tent out of snow, which they call an *igloovigaq*.

Experienced igloo builders can erect a snow tent in about an hour. Usually two men work on the structure, cutting out large blocks of snow with a special snow knife. Blocks are stacked leaning inward until they meet at a curved top reaching twelve feet high. A short tunnel is built to keep the winds out, and often a block of ice is inserted in the wall to allow light in.

Camping on the ice may not sound like motel living, but it can be quite enjoyable. A fire is built on the floor. They don't have water beds, but they spread furs over the ground to create ice beds. The temperature in an igloo reaches seventy degrees, making it as warm as your house. A hole in the top of the snow tent provides an opening for fresh air and allows smoke to escape.

Food is seldom a problem. There are no stores for hundreds of miles, but the seals caught during the day are kept in one corner of the igloo set aside for just that purpose. It doesn't take an Inuit mother long to put a tasty meal together from these supplies. A floor space ten feet across gives an entire family plenty of room to operate.

Time changes most things, so the igloo is now being replaced with modern tents by most Eskimos, but several Inuits prefer the walls of snow. Often they still build them so their children will not forget the ways of their grandparents.

Tents of animal skins, cloth and snow have been a part of the lives of countless millions. In Bible times they liked to think of God as living in a tent. When they spoke of dying and going to live with God, they pictured a magnificent tent with walls made of rare animal hides and the inside decorated with fine trappings. The center of the structure was God and they looked forward to being with Him forever.

By believing in Jesus Christ we each have the promise of spending eternity with God. No one knows what the area might look like, but it could be in a spectacular tent. Maybe even one made of snow.

"I long to dwell in your tent forever" (Ps. 61:4).

1. What does Inuit mean?
2. How is an igloo built?
3. How do you picture a home in heaven?

forty-six

A Mean Wolverine

Trappers claim they must hurry to capture a wolverine. If caught in a steel cage, this 40-pound member of the weasel family will begin to dismantle the trap. When held in a foot trap, it will first try to take the hinges apart and if that fails, it might chew its toes off and leave.

Any animal this tough is soon respected and feared. Some of the stories about them are hard to check for sure. There aren't many wolverines, and during the summer they go up into the mountains of Montana and other areas to avoid people.

Some scientists believe it is basically a shy, quiet creature. But there is no doubt that when the wolverine turns nasty, it is given plenty of room by most animals.

They may not attack large animals every day, but occasionally stories are told of wolverines killing mountain lions, grizzly bears and black bears. If possible, however, a wolverine tries to avoid these huge animals.

One account claims a wolverine has taken the life of a polar bear in battle. Backwoodsmen insist the wolverine knows no fear. When wolverines tear into battle, grunting and slashing, they fight until the death. Razor-sharp teeth and long claws make them champions in most conflicts.

A wolverine's reputation in war is only part of his bad reputation. Trappers insist that the angry animal will try to wreck traps on purpose. Wolverines have been known to eat parts of animals caught in traps and then destroy the rest. It appears that they steal traps and carry them off and hide them.

Because wolverines seem so mean, Eskimos call them the Evil One. Their terrible tempers leave them with few friends. People don't love the idea of protecting the wolverine because its foul temper makes it undesirable.

That same rule carries over to people. Those who are kind and thoughtful are often welcomed, loved and well thought of. The cruel ones are kept at a distance and ignored.

Our behavior has a way of coming back to reward us. Mean people hurt themselves. Good people receive good treatment most of the time.

"A kind man benefits himself, but a cruel man brings himself harm" (Prov. 11:17).

1. Few people see wolverines. Why is this?
2. What do trappers tell us about wolverines?
3. How can you continue to build a good reputation today?

forty-seven

Flapping Their Funny Feet

All of us want to look attractive. That's why we wash our faces and comb our hair. We wear clothes that are clean and usually neatly pressed. Not many of us want to look like something that fell off a garbage truck.

The booby is a bird that has the same interest we have. It wants to look good for other booby birds. After the bird has been flying and is making a landing, the male booby will try to show the females how sharp he looks. While landing he will start flapping his webbed feet. If she sees his feet flashing, she will think he is one special bird.

His feet are special. The red-footed booby will turn the heads of some females, while the blue-footed ones look great to others. To us nonboobies, he seems to be making a goofy landing, but the bird thinks he's cool.

That's how the booby birds got their name. They act like comedians, so they have earned a name that comes from the Spanish word *bobo*, meaning "clown."

When the booby isn't showing off, it spends most of its time in the air searching for food. Floating high above the water it stays ready to dive at the first sight of fish. When it attacks, cutting into the ocean, the booby can swim well enough to actually chase a fish underwater. Grabbing its catch firmly in its beak, the bird struggles to the surface and takes off again. Boobies are fast, strong and skillful.

Their body structures equip the booby especially well for

flight, but they do have some reasons to spend time on the ground. They enjoy raising families in their small, plain nests. When their chicks are first born, the parents remain home to keep their feathered children from wandering away. Other seabirds will steal them if the booby chicks are left unguarded.

Chicks have a natural curiosity and they like to stray off to investigate other nests. While the adventurous spirit is admirable, it's also dangerous. It would be far better for them to stay close and learn from their parents before poking their beaks into places where they might get hurt.

Human beings suffer from the same temptations. We want to get away from home and try things that we know could be harmful. We don't want to listen to anyone. So we keep poking into dangerous situations.

What's it like to shoplift? What will really happen if we climb that fence? If we smoke a cigarette, how will it feel? Nothing will happen if we jump on the back of trucks . . .

Smart people stay close to home, especially while they are young. There is a great deal to learn and we can learn much of it at home. If we are just out looking for trouble, we are sure to find it, no matter how old we are.

"Like a bird that strays from its nest is a man who strays from his home" (Prov. 27:8).

1. What is the origin of the name "booby bird"?
2. Why does the booby bird flap its webbed feet when landing?
3. Why does the Bible tell us to listen to our parents' teaching?

forty-eight

Horseshoe Crabs and Free Rides

They look a little like old army tanks, and each year they invade the shores of the east coast of the United States and Mexico. If you aren't used to them, you wonder what kind of prehistoric monster has crawled out of the sea. Millions of horseshoe crabs make their landing each spring startling some people, amazing others, and aggravating the rest.

There isn't anything quite like a horseshoe crab. We don't even know what to call them. They aren't crabs. If they have relatives, they are spiders and scorpions. Even that's hard to believe since they don't look anything alike.

The average person isn't terribly eager to eat one of these monsters. They are generally used to feed chickens and pigs or are ground up to make fertilizer. Creative Indians made the tails into fishing spears and emptied the shells for use as bowls. It's almost as if no one has known what to do with these green-brown visitors from the sea.

Recently the horseshoe crab has gained greater importance because of its medical contributions. Scientists study their eyes to give us a better understanding of the human eye.

Also known as the King Crab, these awkward creatures have a tough time making it from the sea to dry land. The male, or bull crab, is smaller than its female counterpart. She is over a foot across and better able to climb in and out of the watery holes.

At this critical point in their journey, Mrs. Horseshoe Crab

113

provides free rides. The male clasps his claws to the sides of the female and travels piggyback to the shore. They need each other to keep their life cycle going and aren't too proud to give and accept help.

Stories like this appear frequently in nature. In many cases animals need each other to survive. They provide food, housing, warning calls, bug inspection, transportation, warmth, baby-sitting services and acting lessons. A few make good loners, but most of them realize how dependent they are on other animals.

Most people don't make good loners either. We need free rides, warning calls, and sometimes a little bug inspection. That explains one of the reasons why God created men and women. The great majority of us need each other.

God likes to produce what we need. He's extra good at being thoughtful.

"But for Adam no suitable helper was found. So the Lord God caused the man to fall into a deep sleep; and while he was sleeping, he took one of the man's ribs and closed up the place with flesh" (Gen. 2:20, 21).

1. Are horseshoe crabs actually crabs?
2. How does the male horseshoe crab depend on the female?
3. Who is probably your best helper right now?

forty-nine

Ladybugs in Your Refrigerator

When a ladybug lands on your arm, be careful how you brush it off. We don't want to hurt a friend that helps fight harmful bugs. Ladybugs eat a huge number of aphids, mealybugs, whiteflies, greenbugs and spider mites. Farmers benefit because the red, tan or black bug will make a feast out of corn earworm or cotton leafworm.

These brightly colored bugs are so useful that some people keep them in a jar in their refrigerator. Ladybugs survive well this way because they hibernate. If houseplants are bothered by aphids, the owner can release the chilled bugs in the living room. After the aphids are eaten, the ladybugs are collected and stored back in the cooler.

A member of the beetle family, one ladybug can eat 60 to 300 tiny aphids.

That's only a small part of the way this bug-eater is used to keep nature in balance. Every winter workers are sent into the mountains of the western United States to gather ladybugs while they hibernate. They pick millions and place them in jars. By keeping them at low temperatures, the ladybugs are perfectly safe until they are needed.

When the weather warms up, farmers release these bugs into their fields. Soon they perform the needed job of pest control without using chemicals.

Naturalists have employed ladybugs in apple orchards, potato and sugar beet fields as well as in cornfields. It's easier to use chemicals and probably more dependable, but we may be

ignoring a tremendous resource. God gave a balance to nature and in many ways it will still work best today.

God is in the business of helping. He doesn't look for ways to complicate our lives. He isn't trying to see how difficult He can make it. When we look to Him and ask for help, God loves to give it. He even helps us when we don't ask.

Maybe we would like to calm down and study better. God could help us do that. How would you like to forgive your brother? God could help you be more forgiving. Do you ever have trouble with a bad temper? God could help you quiet that down, too.

Those are only a few examples. God is a full-time helper who wants us to get in contact with Him. And we don't even have to climb a snowcapped mountain with a jar to find Him.

"I lift up my eyes to the hills—where does my help come from? My help comes from the Lord, the Maker of heaven and earth" (Ps. 121:1, 2).

1. How does a ladybug help keep nature in balance?
2. How do ladybugs help farmers?
3. Have you ever kept ladybugs in your refrigerator?

fifty

The Daily Destroyer

Where are the animals that cause the most destruction in nature? If you want an answer, don't look up for a huge animal but look down at the ground for a small one. Ounce for ounce the tiny shrew is one of the greatest destroyers in the world.

Only two inches long in many cases, shrews love to attack, pounce, kill, eat and ruin. They don't hesitate to fight a creature twice their size, and shrews almost always come out the winners.

They look like mice except for their pointed noses and small ears. Each day is devoted entirely to eating. Their favorite food is insects but some varieties love fish. The giant otter shrew of Africa reaches two feet in length and enjoys seafood.

Shrews are driven by an incredible need for food. Every day a shrew will eat enough to equal its own weight. That would be like you shoveling down about a hundred pounds of food daily.

These high-strung nervous bodies have no time to relax. They are constantly chewing. To help defeat their victims, the short-tailed shrews of North America have poisonous saliva. After a couple of quick bites the large insects die rapidly. Shrew poison is similar to that found in cobras.

Normally shrews like to attack butterflies, beetles and slugs, but they have been known to eat rats and snakes. Shrews have a few enemies that like to dine on them, such as great horned owls and bobcats. However, it seems shrews aren't particularly tasty.

Healthy human beings have a pulse rate of 72 beats a minute. If you checked a shrew's pulse it would probably be clipping along at 1,000 beats per minute. That may help explain why its life expectancy is only a year and a half. Because of its constant motion, its racing body apparently burns out.

The entire life of shrews seems to be spent tearing things apart and destroying. They look out for themselves and don't seem to care about anything else. Some people are much like shrews. All of their lives they aim at satisfying their own appetites. They don't think about others or about God.

Christians have wider interests in life. We look out for those in need, we share what we have, and we try to serve God in Jesus Christ. God keeps us from becoming completely selfish.

"Their destiny is destruction, their god is their stomach, and their glory is in their shame. Their mind is on earthly things" (Phil. 3:19).

1. Choose the correct answer: A shrew eats how much food every day? (1) One-half of its weight, (2) Equal to its weight, (3) Twice its weight.
2. Why does a shrew have such a short lifespan?
3. Do you know someone who goes out of his way to help others?

fifty-one

Repeating Parrots

Off the beaten path in southeast Asia, you might be able to locate a small bird hanging upside down like a bat. It is a hanging parrot that has a strange way of sleeping.

If someone mentions a parrot, most of us immediately think of a bird that can talk. That's only a small part of the parrot story. There are three hundred fifteen species of parrots and many of them lead incredible lifestyles. They are colorful and can use their tongues as an extra hand. Pushing their tongue against their beak, parrots can handle objects with amazing ease.

Even their toes are particularly suited for their needs. Two of their toes point backwards, allowing the parrot a good grip on branches.

As with much of nature, the parrot population is in danger as man continues to remove jungles and forests. A few men fight tirelessly to save the parrot. (Some went so far as to glue new flight feathers on an injured parrot. The bird soon flew again with the temporary feathers and after new ones grew back, the men removed the ones they had attached.)

Parrots are frequently bought as pets, but protecting them in the wild will continue to be a difficult job for years to come.

There are two varieties, the African gray parrot and the Amazon green parrot, that seem to learn to talk the easiest. These parrots appear to have the best verbal skills. However, bird lovers say it is not as simple as people think. Training parrots to talk is a slow, patient task. Only after hours of repeating the same words does even the most gifted parrot begin to repeat some of what it hears.

This isn't to suggest that parrots learn a language or can hold a conversation. Rather, it is a crude form of learning to repeat a little bit of what they have heard.

Unfortunately, some parrots have been taught to say terrible, ugly and insulting words. They merely say them without any idea as to what the words mean.

People aren't much better in the things that they say. Often we use some gross and horrible words. They are terms that we have picked up and we repeat without thinking. By using them we may hurt someone's feelings and not realize it.

We are smarter than parrots and can watch what we say. God doesn't want us to throw words around carelessly. Christians can be careful, choosing words that are fun but not harmful.

"Do not let any unwholesome talk come out of your mouths, but only what is helpful for building others up according to their needs, that it may benefit those who listen" (Eph. 4:29).

1. How do parrots use their tongues?
2. How are their toes suited to sitting on branches?
3. Think of a way you will control what you say today.

fifty-two

Never Hug a Grizzly

If you are looking for something soft and cuddly to hug, forget the grizzly bear. The cubs look like friendly pets, but they grow to be some of the toughest animals in nature.

The small grizzlies roam in the United States—mostly in Montana, Idaho, Wyoming and Colorado. They grow to be 8 feet tall and weigh 800 pounds. However, the ones in Alaska and Canada get almost twice that heavy. They only reach nine feet tall, but they would crush many scales at 1,800 pounds.

It would be fun to hug a grizzly, but not so fun if it hugged you back.

Their claws stretch out to 4 sharp inches. They can run at the impressive speed of 15 to 20 miles per hour. However, some have been clocked at 35 miles per hour. Fortunately, the grizzlies aren't supposed to be able to climb trees—but their cubs can.

Normally, the grizzly can live to be from 30 to 40 years old. In a zoo atmosphere they have reached as old as 50 years.

If you did have a huge grizzly as a pet, it wouldn't be hard to feed. It eats practically anything and everything. Scientists call a grizzly bear omnivorous, which means it eats both vegetables and meat.

In the winter these bears like to sleep, not only because they have so much trouble finding food, but also because before they go to sleep they eat some kinds of foods that make them sleep a long time. They might wake up after a month of snoozing, hunt around for a snack and head back to bed. The grizzly at the Henry Doorly Zoo in Omaha, Nebraska, doesn't take a long winter nap. It gets plenty of food and stays awake.

The workers at Yellowstone National Park and Glacier National Park are trying to protect the number of grizzlies, but the job is difficult. Bears don't mix well with people. Often they eat garbage left by campers and backpackers. That leads to battles between the bears and the visitors. Fortunately they don't fight often. In almost 90 years grizzly bears have killed only 14 people in the lower 48 states.

Naturally a few people will disagree about grizzlies being pets. There are some which have been trained and kept, but not many.

Because grizzlies eat meat, the sheepherders near the parks and mountains are not fond of bears. The grizzlies don't know enough to stay away, and the ranchers must find some means to protect their livestock.

Fortunately, this problem will not always exist. Someday, after Jesus Christ returns, the grizzly bear and livestock will be able to roam in the same field and live together. Then we will all exist together in peace as God intended.

"The cow will feed with the bear, their young will lie down together, and the lion will eat straw like the ox" (Isa. 11:7).

1. Tell some facts about where grizzlies live and their size.
2. Why do grizzlies sleep in the winter?
3. What will it be like when Jesus Christ returns?